Knights of Pythias, William Blancbois

A Digest of the Laws of the Order of Knights of Pythias

in the state of Pennsylvania

Knights of Pythias, William Blancbois

A Digest of the Laws of the Order of Knights of Pythias
in the state of Pennsylvania

ISBN/EAN: 9783337291303

Printed in Europe, USA, Canada, Australia, Japan

Cover: Foto ©Andreas Hilbeck / pixelio.de

More available books at **www.hansebooks.com**

A

𝕯igest of the 𝕷aws

OF THE ORDER OF

IGHTS OF PYTHIAS

IN THE

State of Pennsylvania.

COMPILED AND PUBLISHED

AUTHORITY OF THE GRAND LODGE OF PENNSYLVANIA,

BY

WILLIAM BLANCBOIS, P. G. C.

PHILADELPHIA:
KNIGHTS OF PYTHIAS JOURNAL PRINT.
1872.

PHILADELPHIA, *Sept.* 1, 1872.

WILLIAM A. M. LOVE, ESQ.,

Chairman of the Committee on Law:

SIR AND BROTHER:

At the semi-annual session of the Grand Lodge of the Knights of Pythias of Pennsylvania, held July 25, 1872, at Wilkesbarre, the following among other proceedings were had, to wit:

Whereas, The Committee on Law have reported to this Grand Lodge that Past Grand Chancellor William Blancbois has prepared a compilation and classification of the Decisions made by this Grand Lodge, and have recommended that he publish the same in book form:

Resolved, That Past Grand Chancellor William Blancbois be requested to submit his said compilation to the Committee on Law, and that said Committee be requested to examine and compare the same, and finding the same correct, thereupon to authenticate the same with their signature, after which Past Grand Chancellor William Blancbois is requested to publish the same, in book form, for sale among the brother-hood, and with the sanction of this Grand Lodge.

In testimony whereof, I have hereunto set my hand and affixed the seal of the Grand Lodge, year and date as above written.

Fraternally yours,

[SEAL.]   GEORGE HAWKES,

Grand Recording and Corresponding Scribe.

GRAND LODGE OF PENNSYLVANIA, K. OF P.

OFFICE OF THE

Chairman of Committee on Law and Supervision.

PHILADELPHIA, *Sept.* 4, 1872.

By request of the Grand Lodge of the State of Pennsylvania, and in accordance with the foregoing resolution, the Committee on Law and Supervision have examined and compared the compilation of Decisions herein contained, and find them to be correct.

WILLIAM A. M. LOVE, No. 22,
JAMES L. POYNTON, No. 11,
DAVID W. WILSON, No. 18,
JOHN B. MERRITT, No. 25,
HERMAN HEROLD, No. 133,
Committee on Law and Supervision.

TO THE KNIGHTHOOD AT LARGE.

In pursuance of a resolution passed by the Grand Lodge of Pennsylvania, at the semi-annual session, held at Wilkesbarre, July 25, 1872, the undersigned submitted the following Digest to the Committee on Law for inspection. At the earnest solicitation of many members of the Order from different jurisdictions, and of the Committee on Law of the Grand Lodge of Pennsylvania, this little work has been compiled, with great care. It comprises all the decisions (not repealed) of the different Grand Chancellors of Pennsylvania; those made by the Committees on Law, and indorsed by the Grand Lodge; and the different resolutions passed by the Grand Lodge; also, the Constitution of Subordinate Lodges, and the Constitution and By-Laws of the Grand Lodge, and selections from Cushing's Manual, as well as other useful information to the membership.

The Committee on Law having approved of the work, it is respectfully dedicated to the brotherhood, by the compiler, with the hope that it may be of some assistance to officers of Lodges and others.

Fraternally, in F., C. and B.,
WILLIAM BLANCBOIS.

PHILADELPHIA, *September 25, 1872.*

DIGEST OF THE LAWS

OF THE

KNIGHTS OF PYTHIAS,

OF THE

STATE OF PENNSYLVANIA.

ABSENCE.

1. Absence from the regular stated meetings of the Lodge for not less than three consecutive evenings or sessions, without lawful excuse, forfeits the right of any officer to the position he holds: *Provided*, The Lodge notifies such officer to appear and show cause why his seat shall not be vacated.

2. Should an officer elect be absent on the night of installation, unless a satisfactory excuse be given for his non-attendance, the installing officer may require the Lodge to immediately elect another member in place of the absentee, and proceed to install him in the office.

3. An officer of a Lodge who is absent, on account of sickness, for a majority of the nights of his term, does not thereby forfeit the honors of the office.

2 (13)

ABSENCE.

4. A subordinate Lodge cannot grant an elective officer leave of absence for the majority of the nights of a term without working a forfeiture of the honors of the term to the officer to whom such leave of absence is granted. Absence caused by sickness is provided for by the Constitution, and the officer is relieved from any penalties for absence caused thereby.

5. A Lodge being unable to hold a meeting for want of a quorum, occasioned by the absence of one or more officers, and the By-Laws providing for a fine in case of such absence, the proper mode of proceeding is for the Recording Scribe, or, in his absence, for any member present, to note the absentees, keep a minute of those who are in attendance, and at the next stated meeting of the Lodge present this record and have it read; this will establish the fact of the absence of certain officers, and justify the Lodge in imposing the fine.

ADJOURNMENT.

6. The Worthy Chancellor cannot entertain a motion to adjourn until the regular order of business, as laid down for the government of Lodges, has been gone through with. When this has been done, and no member offers any

ADJOURNMENT.

matter for the consideration of the Lodge, the Worthy Chancellor will proceed with the closing ceremonies without a motion.

AMENDMENTS.

7. After an amendment to a question, or an amendment to an amendment, has been either adopted or rejected, either of them is susceptible of other amendments. But no amendment to the question, or amendment to the amendment, can be entertained which will destroy that which has already been adopted. Nor can an amendment be again received which has been rejected, unless such amendment be first reconsidered.

8. Every amendment to an amendment must first be decided, previous to others being entertained, as only two amendments are allowed at one time to a question. Therefore, the second amendment must be disposed of previous to entertaining other amendments.

APPEALS.

9. A member considering that injustice has been done him by the decision of the Lodge, may present to the Lodge, within one month thereafter, a written appeal, setting forth his

APPEALS.

reasons, and the Lodge, during the succeeding month, shall send the appeal, together with the journal and testimony taken by the Committee, and a copy of all the minutes of the Lodge relating to the subject, certified by the signatures of the Worthy Chancellor, Recording Scribe, and seal of the Lodge, to the Grand Chancellor. The appellant shall also furnish the Grand Chancellor with a copy of his appeal, and proof of service upon the Lodge, within the time specified. In default thereof, the appeal may be dismissed to the disadvantage of the Lodge or brother neglecting to attend to the matter.

10. When an appeal from the decision of the Worthy Chancellor upon a by-law is before the Lodge, the Vice Chancellor, during the pending of an appeal, is virtually the presiding officer, and as such must decide all points of order that may be raised, and the appeal must be proceeded with and settled before any other business can be transacted.

11. No appeal from the decision of the Worthy Chancellor upon a question of law arising under the Constitution can be submitted to a Lodge for its decision, as the Lodge did not make, nor can it construe it; the only appeal being to the Grand Lodge, the Grand Chancel-

APPEALS.

lor, or the District Deputy Grand Chancellor, as the case may be.

12. Any one member may appeal from the decision of the Worthy Chancellor on a question of order.

13. A counsellor in an appeal case must be a member of the Order in good standing, and neither the counsel nor a Committee from a Lodge can be acknowledged by the Committee on Appeals unless they present proper credentials from the Lodge, attested by the Worthy Chancellor and Recording Scribe, and with the seal of the Lodge.

14. When an appeal is taken from the decision of a subordinate Lodge to the Grand Chancellor, or to a District Deputy Grand Chancellor, the decision of the Lodge stands as the judgment in the case, until it is reversed by the higher authority.

APPOINTMENTS.

15. The Worthy Chancellor cannot appoint the Guide of the Lodge to fill the chair of Vice Chancellor in his (the Vice Chancellor's) absence, and when there are Past Chancellors in the room.

ARREARS.

16. A member disabled or taken sick, when three months or more in arrears for dues, cannot, by the payment of such arrears, become. beneficial during such sickness or disability; nor would his competent relatives be entitled to funeral benefits, in the event of death from such sickness or disability; and the expiration of the penalty for non-payment of dues does not relieve a brother who becomes sick while in arrears; nor does it entitle him to sick benefits, or his competent relatives to funeral benefits, should he die from said illness.

17. A brother while sick and receiving benefits from his Lodge cannot become in arrears so as to be debarred from receiving benefits on that account, as it is the duty of the Lodge to deduct from the amount drawn for his benefits, and have placed to his credit a sufficient sum to keep him in good standing.

18. A member in arrears for dues, three months or more, is debarred from receiving weekly benefits, and is required to undergo the penalty as provided in the By-Laws, after all arrears are paid in *full*, before he becomes entitled to benefits. Payment of arrears and expiration of penalty does not entitle a brother, who

ARREARS.

was in arrears when he became sick, to weekly benefits.

19. A brother three months or more in arrears for *dues*, who pays the same or any portion thereof, reducing the sum of his indebtedness less than three months dues, is entitled to the S. A. P. W., can vote, speak, or be a candidate, and hold office in the Lodge.

20. A brother who pays up his arrears when indisposed, and yet able to attend to his usual business, would be entitled to benefits should such indisposition terminate in sickness. The term sickness, within the meaning of the law relative to payment of arrearages while sick or disabled, implies a state of health which prevents one from attending to his ordinary vocation.

21. Should the Financial Scribe neglect to credit a member for money paid as dues *in the Lodge*, and the brother thereby become in arrears on the books, the error of the Financial Scribe in keeping the accounts cannot be made to result to his disadvantage and injury, as a Lodge cannot take advantage of its own wrong or that of its officers when acting in their official capacity.

22. A member in arrears to the amount of

ARREARS.

one year's dues may be suspended from membership, and shall not be restored until he has paid such sum as the By-Laws of his Lodge may prescribe.

23. If a member whose appeal or grievance is before his Lodge, or a Committee thereof, the Grand Lodge or its Committee, becomes a year in arrears for dues, he is not liable to suspension for non-payment of dues.

24. Every member neglecting to pay, and in arrears to the Lodge to the amount of three months dues or more, shall not be entitled to vote, be disqualified for any office, and stand suspended from all benefits and privileges during the pleasure of the Lodge.

25. A member in arrears for three months dues or more is ineligible for nomination for office, and cannot, by paying his arrearages, subsequently qualify himself for election.

ASSESSMENTS.

26. A Lodge cannot make and enforce the payment of any assessments, as the Constitution does not recognize them.

AUDITING COMMITTEE.

27. On the night of election of officers there

AUDITING COMMITTEE.

shall be appointed a Committee of three Knights in good standing, for the purpose of auditing the books and settling the accounts of the Recording Scribe, Financial Scribe, and Banker. Said Committee to report at the next stated meeting in writing. The Worthy Chancellor shall appoint the majority, and the Vice Chancellor the minority of the above Committee.

BALLOT.

28. A ballot properly taken, that results in the election or rejection of a candidate for membership, "cannot be reconsidered" by the Lodge, neither can the Worthy Chancellor treat it as if not taken. The consent of the Grand Lodge must first be procured before a reballot can be had in such cases.

29. It being discovered, after balloting for and electing a candidate, that fraud and falsehood were resorted to in presenting his name to the Lodge, the ballot may be declared void and a new ballot had, provided two-thirds of the members present so decide.

30. Balloting, by ball or ticket, is a secret mode of voting, and so designed in order that the vote of one member should not influence that of another, but that every one should vote ac-

BALLOT.

cording to the dictates of his own conscience, free from external influence; and it is a violation of the laws and principles of the Order to go into an investigation as to how a member voted.

31. At the close of a ballot, on balloting for candidates, the Guide must present the box to the Vice Chancellor, who shall inspect the vote and announce the same to the Worthy Chancellor, viz.: " The ballot is in favor of the applicant," or " The ballot is unfavorable to the applicant," as the case may be. The Guide will then present the box to the Venerable Patriarch, who will inspect the vote and confirm the announcement, if correct. The Guide will then present the box to the Worthy Chancellor, who will inspect the vote and proclaim the result to the Lodge and its effect upon the application.

32. In a ballot upon the report of a Committee on the application of a member, suspended for non-payment of dues, to be reinstated, two-thirds of the valid votes cast are necessary to reinstate.

33. Upon the receipt by the Lodge of the report of an investigating Committee on a candidate, whether favorable or unfavorable, a ballot must be taken.

BALLOT.

34. It is the inherent right of every brother Knight in good standing to deposit his ballot according to the dictates of his conscience. But no brother has the right to form a conspiracy to reject good men, in urging other brothers to deposit their ballots against applicants, to retard the progress of the Lodge and the Order, in order that his selfish ends may be accomplished.

35. If a brother's conscience dictates that he is depositing his ballot for the best interests of the Lodge and the Order, he is right. But if for any selfish or vindictive motive, he is working against the best interests of the Lodge and the Order.

36. If a brother should so far forget himself as to boast that it was his intention to deposit ballots against an applicant or applicants for membership, and would urge others to assist him, he is liable to have charges preferred against him, and, after due trial and conviction, be fined or suspended, as the Lodge may determine.

37. Upon the examination of a ballot it is not necessary for the Worthy Chancellor to state the number cast; he merely announces the result, favorable or unfavorable, as the case may be.

BANKER.

38. The Banker shall be elected annually at the time prescribed by the Constitution.

39. He shall receive from the Financial Scribe all moneys received by him for the Lodge, and give his receipt therefor. A neglect of this duty, and a loss to the Lodge occurring thereby, the Banker would be responsible.

40. He shall keep a correct account of all moneys so received, and make no disbursements thereof unless authorized by an order from the Worthy Chancellor, attested by the Recording Scribe.

BENEFITS.

41. A member cannot rightfully claim weekly benefits when disabled by any disease or infirmity by which he was afflicted previous to his initiation or admission in the Lodge; or for any sickness or other disability originating from intemperance, vicious or immoral conduct; or while charges are pending against him under the penal provisions of the laws, but when he has been exonerated or acquitted, after due trial, he may claim for the time if otherwise entitled; or when so disabled as to prevent him following his usual occupation, but able to pursue some other business.

BENEFITS.

42. Every member who has passed the probationary period fixed in the By-Laws, and received the Knight's degree, incapacitated by sickness or other disability from attending to his usual business or some other occupation, shall be considered a beneficial member, entitled to receive such weekly benefits as the By-Laws prescribe, (not less than two dollars per week:) *Provided always, however,* That his disability is not of a permanent character, and such as does not prevent other men, similarly afflicted, from pursuing their avocations, and that he is in good standing in the Lodge.

43. The Lodge may classify its dues and benefits above the minimum rates specified, prescribe the probationary period to expire previous to a member's becoming beneficial, and fix the time when weekly benefits shall commence to be paid to its sick and disabled members by laws of general application; and upon satisfactory evidence that its funds are so reduced as to be unable to meet the legitimate demands upon its treasury, may be allowed a dispensation authorizing it to reduce its weekly benefits to a sum not less than one dollar per week.

44. It is not required of a sick brother to

3

BENEFITS.

notify the Lodge that he is going away on a visit. If he should go and remain four weeks, he would then have to make application the same as other brothers who reside three (3) miles or more from the place of meeting.

45. If the Lodge has any doubt of the brother's sickness while absent, they may require a certificate from the physician who attended him while absent. But if the Lodge is satisfied that the brother was unable to attend to his usual or some other business, and was in good standing, the Lodge should pay him his benefits.

46. Absent members, desirous of claiming benefits, shall write or cause to be written an application to their Lodge for benefits within four weeks from the commencement of such sickness or disability; if on land, to be attested as the Constitution requires, and if at sea, to be attested by the surgeon of the ship or vessel, and if there be no surgeon, by the captain or mate, to be forwarded to his Lodge at the earliest opportunity. If the first application should be delayed, and the second should arrive before the first, the Lodge should pay the brother, as it would be rightfully due him: *Provided*, That the application be not antedated to cover time

BENEFITS.

embraced in a previous application, and that the postmark and date of application be satisfactory to the Lodge.

47. It is not necessary for a beneficial member, when sick, to ask for benefits, the Relief Committee visiting him; it is the duty of the Relief Committee to wait on him until he has recovered or deceased, and pay him his benefits when due, within forty-eight hours after the close of each meeting.

48. If a brother reinstated is taken sick, or disabled while serving out a penalty prescribed in the By-Laws for the non-payment of dues, (if otherwise entitled,) at the expiration of the time specified he becomes a beneficiary, entitled to the same benefits and privileges as other members.

49. A brother disqualified by the Constitution or By-Laws from receiving weekly benefits: a Lodge cannot evade the spirit of the law by the enactment of a by-law rendering such disqualified member entitled to a weekly donation, as it would then, under another name, give him a weekly claim upon the funds of the Lodge, which claim is denied by the Constitution.

50. A misrepresentation made by a member

BENEFITS.

as to his age at the time of his initiation and discovered by the Lodge only after his death, would be a bar to the claim of his widow or competent relatives for funeral benefits.

51. If a Knight afflicted with temporary insanity, and in a deranged condition of mind, destroys his life, his competent relatives are entitled to funeral benefits; except where the disease and destruction of life has been produced by dissipated habits or immoral conduct, when they would not be entitled.

52. It is not legal for a Lodge to pass a law to pay funeral benefits to "Legal Representatives" or "Executors and Administrators." The operations of such a By-Law would allow funeral benefits to go into the estate of a deceased brother, and be made liable for the payment of his debts. Funeral benefits are not intended for this purpose, but for the relief of his family, and purposely to aid them in giving their relative a proper burial.

53. The Relief Committee must pay the funeral benefits to the nearest competent relative, provided the Worthy Chancellor is satisfied that such relative will apply the money faithfully to the purpose specified; otherwise the

BENEFITS.

Worthy Chancellor shall apply the money for such purpose, and return the surplus, if any, to the Financial Scribe, with receipts for the expenses incurred.

54. Where the By-Laws of a Lodge require that applications for benefits shall be made according to a prescribed form in writing, and a brother is too ill to write, and a friend informs the Lodge, or a proper officer thereof, orally of the fact, the benefits must be paid if the brother is otherwise qualified.

55. A Lodge cannot make it a condition of the reinstatement of a suspended member that he shall never receive benefits.

56. Should a brother, in good standing at the time of his death, be indebted to the Lodge for fines or dues, it must be deducted from his funeral benefits.

57. A brother, having drawn weekly benefits from his Lodge, through mistake of the proper officers, before he was legally entitled, and when informed of the fact, having promised to return the same, but failing to do so, the Lodge may, at any subsequent sickness of said brother, reimburse itself by retaining an amount equal to that paid to said brother as above.

BENEFITS.

58. A brother in good standing, whose wife dies through intemperance or from the effects of other vicious habits, is entitled to the funeral benefits as prescribed in the By-Laws.

59. A brother who attempts suicide while temporarily insane, and thereby incapacitates himself for work, is entitled to weekly benefits, provided his insanity arises from any natural cause or disease.

60. A Lodge may enact a by-law specifying that a brother entitled to weekly benefits shall not receive the same for the first week's sickness.

BLANKS.

61. When a blank is to be filled, the question shall be first taken upon the smallest sum or number, and the longest and latest time proposed.

BUSINESS.

62. All the business in a subordinate Lodge, except conferring of degrees, shall be transacted in the Knight's degree.

BY-LAWS.

63. By-Laws in conformity with the Consti-

BY-LAWS.

tution may be made, altered, amended, added to, or dispensed with, by submitting the proposition to the Lodge in writing, signed by two members of the Knight's degree, and having it read at two stated meetings previous to being acted upon, when, two-thirds of the valid votes cast concurring, it shall be adopted: *Provided, however*, It does not contravene or conflict with any of the established principles, laws, rules, or regulations of the Grand Lodge, the Supreme Lodge of the Knights of Pythias, or the Order in general; but they shall have neither force nor effect until approved by the Grand Chancellor, and all By-Laws or parts of By-Laws, which have been adopted by the Lodge, contravening or conflicting therewith, shall be considered as repealed from and after the date of such approval.

64. Subordinate Lodges wishing their By-Laws approved must furnish the Committee on Law with not less than five printed copies, properly attested; an approved copy of the By-Laws of each Lodge to be forwarded, and kept in the office of the Grand Scribe.

65. The By-Laws of subordinate Lodges, or amendments thereto, require the sanction of the Committee on Law of the Grand Lodge, and of the Grand Chancellor, before they go into effect.

BY-LAWS.

66. It is perfectly legal for a Lodge to have a by-law compelling a brother to sit up with a sick member, or pay a fine if he fails to do so.

67. A by-law not in accordance with the Constitution, general laws, or usages of the Order, although it may have inadvertently received the sanction of the Committee on Law and the Grand Chancellor, must cease to be operative whenever the Lodge is officially informed of the fact.

68. The Grand Lodge may alter or amend such part or parts of its By-Laws as two-thirds of the Lodges present entitled to vote may determine, providing such alterations or amendments do not conflict with the Constitution, and have been proposed at a regular session previous to adoption.

69. A Lodge cannot set aside any part of their By-Laws by a mere resolution.

CARDS.

70. Any member squaring his account on the books of the Lodge may apply for a withdrawal card, when a vote shall be taken, and in case the majority of those voting refuse to grant the card, the objections shall be stated in writing,

CARDS.

and the applicant be entitled to a trial in the same manner and form as upon other charges.

71. The vote of the majority in favor of granting a withdrawal card severs the connection of the applicant from the Lodge, whether the card is taken or not.

72. A card may be recalled or annulled by the Lodge *for proper cause.*

73. Members of a defunct Lodge, who were in good standing at the time of dissolution, may be admitted into another Lodge, after having applied for and received a card, signed by the Grand Chancellor, and countersigned by the Grand Recording and Corresponding Scribe, with the seal of the Grand Lodge attached; the application for such card must be accompanied by the fee of two dollars, the card to hold good for twelve months.

74. A brother having lost his withdrawal card, and wishing to connect himself again with the Order, may apply for a duplicate card to the Lodge from which he withdrew, when, upon satisfactory evidence received by the Lodge of the brother's identity, the duplicate may be granted.

75. The Grand Recording and Corresponding Scribe is authorized to furnish blank with-

CARDS.

drawal cards to the Representative or Recording Scribe of a subordinate Lodge, upon application therefor.

76. It is not legal for any subordinate Lodge to enact a by-law preventing any brother Knight from depositing his card in such Lodge, by reason of his being over fifty years of age.

77. The vote on granting a withdrawal card is the usual voting sign, and is merely taken to ascertain if there be objections to the granting of the card. Should a majority of the legal voters present vote against granting the card, or there be objections, they must be reduced to writing, and submitted to the Lodge at the same session; otherwise the Worthy Chancellor, before the Lodge closes the session, must declare the card granted.

78. A withdrawal card entitles the holder thereof to the S. A. P. W. in force at the time the card is issued, and the card can be visited on during the period, and until the S. A. P. W. thus given expires, and *no longer ;* but the card may be presented for application to membership at *any* time before or after the term of twelve months, as expressed upon the card.

CARDS.

79. A member of the Order wishing to join a Lodge by depositing his withdrawal card from the Lodge of which he was formerly a member, and being elected, but failing to present himself to the Lodge until some time thereafter, on account of absence from the place of meeting, the dues of a member so situated do not commence until he signs the Constitution.

80. Blank withdrawal cards are furnished to subordinates by the Grand Lodge, none others being legal.

CEREMONIES.

81. The Lodge cannot deviate in the ceremonies from the instructions given by the Committee of Superintendence.

82. The ceremony of installation must be performed in the Knight's degree.

CHARGE BOOKS.

83. The charge books of a subordinate Lodge are in the official keeping of the Worthy Chancellor. He shall neither take nor allow them to be taken from the Lodge-room; he shall place them in a secure place (which must be provided by the Lodge) immediately after the close of each session, and no copies of or ex-

CHARGE BOOKS.

tracts from any part or parts of the books shall be taken for any purpose whatever; and no officer or member, except the Worthy Chancellor, or in his absence the Vice Chancellor or Guide, shall be intrusted with the key of the receptacle for the said books; and any other officer or member opening the same subjects himself to charges, and is liable to suspension.

CHARGES.

84. Charges or complaints made against members of the Lodge, under the penal provisions of the laws, rules, and regulations, shall be reduced to writing, and distinctly state the cause, time, and place of occurrence, and the Recording Scribe shall furnish the accused with a copy thereof and notice that the matter will be taken up for consideration at the next stated meeting of the Lodge, one week thereafter, when a Committee of five members, of the Knight's degree, shall be appointed.

85. The Committee to whom a charge has been referred shall examine the parties, their proofs and witnesses, carefully and impartially, after giving them notice and fair opportunity to be present at the time specified, when the accused and accuser each have the privilege of

CHARGES.

being represented by a member of the Order in good standing, having the Knight's degree; but no witness or person other than the accused and accuser, their representatives, and the Committee, shall be allowed to be present during the examination; and the Committee shall keep a correct journal of the proceedings, reduce the testimony received to writing, and have it signed by the witnesses in the order it was received, and, after having received all the evidence and proofs presented, reduce their opinion as to the guilt or innocence of the accused to writing, and present the same, together with the journal of their proceedings and the testimony received, to the Lodge, at a stated meeting, as early as practicable thereafter.

86. It is the duty of a brother taken sick while under charges to report himself to the Lodge, and the Relief Committee must visit him.

87. Charges preferred against a District Deputy Grand Chancellor, in regard to his official acts, must be preferred in the Grand Lodge. As to his acts as a member of the Order, the proper tribunal is the subordinate Lodge.

88. A Committee on Charges having made their report to the Lodge, at the next stated

CHARGES.

meeting the same shall be considered and a ballot taken, (the white balls in favor and the black opposed,) when the majority of the ballots cast being in favor of the report, it shall be recorded as the judgment of the Lodge.

89. When an impeached Lodge neglects or refuses to answer within a given time, it may be tried, suspended or dissolved for contempt.

90. A Lodge is required to entertain a charge against one of its members when brought by a member of another Lodge, if the said charge is in regular form, properly attested, and thought worthy of investigation by the Lodge to which the brother making the charge belongs.

91. All members present are required to vote upon the report of a Committee on Charges, and upon the penalty to be imposed, except those whose interests are involved in the result.

92. Any member of a Lodge who has been regularly tried upon a charge containing several counts, and acquitted, cannot be again tried upon that charge, or any of the separate counts therein contained.

93. A member under penal charges cannot be refused admittance to the Lodge, and may

CHARGES.

participate in the work of the Lodge. If an officer of the Lodge, he may continue to perform the functions of his office, unless the Lodge decides otherwise; the only effect of undecided charges being to deprive him of the right to be installed into an office, or take a withdrawal card, and where the charges bear upon the right to benefits, to suspend the payment thereof until a final decision is given.

94. When a charge is regularly preferred against an officer *elect* before installation, the incumbent must hold over, filling the chair *pro tem.* until the result of the trial upon the charge is known, when, if proven guilty, and the penalty is simply a fine, the officer elect may be installed on its payment; but a *suspension* will cause a vacancy which must be filled by a new election.

95. When charges are preferred under the penal provisions of the law by one brother against another, they must be reduced to writing, with the signature of the brother attached who preferred the charges.

96. It requires no action of the Lodge to receive charges regularly made. It is the duty of the Worthy Chancellor to receive them, in

CHARGES.

justice to the brother preferring them, if he be in good standing, the brother being responsible for the same under the law; the Worthy Chancellor shall direct the Recording Scribe to read the charges to the Lodge, after which the whole matter lies over until the next stated meeting, the Recording Scribe furnishing the accused with a copy of the charges, and notice that they will be taken up for consideration at the next stated meeting of the Lodge; when a Committee of five will be appointed, as the By-Laws of the Lodge may direct, the Committee to proceed in accordance with the law as laid down in the Constitution.

97. When the Worthy Chancellor receives charges, regularly preferred under the penal provisions of the law, they become the property of the Lodge, the accused and the accuser, and cannot be withdrawn without the consent of the three parties above named; and if the Lodge and the accuser should withdraw them without the consent of the accused, they would be doing great injustice to the brother charged, as an accusation has been made against his character, and it is but just and right that he should have a fair, just, and impartial trial, if he demand it.

CHARGES.

98. Charges may be preferred for cause against a sick member who is absent from the place of location of the Lodge, but they cannot be tried in his absence; the brother charged must have a fair opportunity to be present at the trial, either in person or by counsel.

99. A Committee on Charges having been appointed, and before proceeding to a trial, a member of said Committee notifies the Lodge of his inability to serve on account of absence from the city, town, or borough, the Lodge must proceed to fill the vacancy in the manner in which the Committee was originally selected.

100. It is *not* the official duty of any officer of a Lodge to prefer charges against a member on information given by persons not members of the Order; but in case such information is given by a creditable person, the officer should communicate the subject-matter of it to the Lodge for its consideration and action.

101. The Worthy Chancellor or Vice Chancellor of a Lodge, preferring a charge against a member, are not competent to appoint the Committee to try the case, or sit as officers when said charge is under consideration, and the Lodge must select a Committee by ballot, unless the

CHARGES.

By-Laws provide a way of selection other than the appointment by the Worthy Chancellor or Vice Chancellor.

102. A Committee investigating charges against a brother must exclude all persons from the room except the parties to the trial, and admit and examine the witnesses separately.

103. A brother, pleading guilty in open Lodge to a charge preferred against him, waives a trial; but the Committee appointed to try the case may present a resolution prescribing the punishment for the offence.

104. In the ballot upon the report of a Committee on Charges, as to the guilt or innocence of the accused, a majority decides.

105. In balloting to prescribe the punishment to be inflicted on a member found guilty of a charge, it requires a two-thirds vote to reprimand, fine, or suspend.

CHARTER.

106. Not less than nine Knights in good standing, sound in health, mind, limb, and body, not less than twenty-one years of age, may apply to the Grand Lodge for a charter or dispensation to establish a new Lodge, which application

CHARTER.

must be accompanied by a sum of not less than fifteen dollars, exclusive of the printed Ritual of the Order, which shall be furnished at such prices as the Grand Lodge may determine: *Provided, however*, That in places where the Order is not established, it is not necessary for the applicants to be Knights. The application must be accompanied by the withdrawal cards from the former Lodge.

107. A Lodge may be suspended or dissolved, and its charter or dispensation forfeited to the Grand Lodge, for improper conduct; for neglecting or refusing to conform to the Constitution or laws of the Grand Lodge, or the general laws, rules, and regulations of the Order; for neglecting or refusing to make its returns, or for non-payment of dues to the Grand Lodge; for neglecting to hold regular stated meetings as provided, unless prevented from doing so by some unforeseen circumstance; by its membership diminishing to less than a constitutional quorum.

108. The charter or dispensation shall not be forfeited until the Lodge has been duly notified of its offence by the Grand Recording and Corresponding Scribe, and opportunity given to answer the charges made against it.

CHARTER.

109. No Lodge shall have power to keep their charter books open for a longer period than three months, unless by special permission from the Grand Lodge or the Grand Chancellor; but in no case shall such permission be granted to any Lodge which has two hundred and fifty members.

COMMITTEES OF GRAND LODGE.

110. The Committee on Law and Supervision shall, when such subjects are presented to the Grand Lodge and duly referred to them, inquire into all cases of infraction of the established laws and regulations of the Order, and recommend such measures as they may deem expedient for correcting the innovation. During the investigation, said Committee shall be actuated by impartial justice alone, and a strict adherence to the Constitution. They shall examine the By-Laws of all subordinate Lodges before being printed, reject any article or section which may conflict with the Constitution, and present them to the Grand Chancellor for approval, before returning them to subordinate Lodges. The Committee shall consist of five members.

111. The Committee of Finance and Mileage

COMMITTEES OF GRAND LODGE.

shall audit the accounts of the Grand Scribe and Grand Banker once in each term, and report their proceedings at each regular meeting, or whenever they may be required to do so by the Grand Lodge. They shall examine all bills presented against the Grand Lodge, and approve the same, prior to an order being drawn for their payment; submit, at each annual meeting, a full estimate of the expenditures of the ensuing year, and also an inventory of all property owned or claimed by the Grand Lodge; compute the mileage of officers and Representatives, and report the amount to which each is entitled, and no order shall be drawn for such amount until the bill for the same is indorsed by a majority of the Committee. It shall consist of seven members.

112. The Committee on Appeals and Grievances shall hear all appeals and grievances from Lodges or members of Lodges referred to them by the Grand Lodge or Grand Chancellor, and report their decisions with the utmost despatch to the Grand Lodge, or to the Grand Chancellor during the recess. But no member of this Committee shall serve on any case of appeal from the Lodge of which he is a member. It shall consist of five members.

COMMITTEES OF GRAND LODGE.

113. The Committee on Returns and Credentials shall examine and report to the Grand Lodge on the regularity of returns of subordinates, and upon the correctness of certificates of Representatives and Past Chancellors. It shall consist of three members.

114. The Committee on Printing and Supplies shall have charge of and superintend all the printing, binding, and supplies which may be from time to time ordered by the Grand Lodge, and make a report to the Grand Lodge of their transactions at each stated session. It shall consist of three members.

115. The Committee of Superintendence shall consist of thirteen members, residing within the limits of the city of Philadelphia. They shall effect an organization within three weeks from the time of their appointment, by the selection of proper officers, (provided, the first person named on the Committee shall act as Chairman,) visit officially each subordinate Lodge in the city of Philadelphia at least twice in each term, for the purpose of instructing in the unwritten work of the Order, and endeavoring to secure uniformity in the same, and report from time to time to the Grand Chancellor. Each member of

COMMITTEES OF GRAND LODGE.

the Committee shall be furnished with a certificate of his appointment, by the Grand Corresponding and Recording Scribe, under his hand and the seal of the Grand Lodge.

116. The Committee on the State of the Order shall consist of five Representatives, to whom shall be referred all appeals from subordinate Lodges for aid and assistance.

117. All Committees shall be appointed from the qualified Representatives, and every Representative neglecting to attend to the duties assigned to the Committee, after being duly notified, shall be dealt with as the Grand Lodge may determine.

118. The first Representative named on a Committee shall be the Chairman thereof; it shall be his duty to convene the Committee within ten days of receiving notice of their appointment, unless otherwise provided for, and proceed to the consideration of the matter or subject, or the discharge of the duties that have been assigned to them.

119. Every Committee shall have authority and power to call for such books, documents, papers, and other articles as are necessary to a correct understanding of the matter or subject

COMMITTEES OF GRAND LODGE.

under consideration or the business they have been charged with.

120. The report of a Committee shall be made in writing and signed by the majority of its members, but the minority or individual members thereof shall be entitled to present their views and conclusions in writing.

121. The Committee on Appeals cannot receive new evidence, except to prove irregularity, informality, or unfairness in the proceedings of a Lodge or its Committee; nor can a Lodge introduce testimony to contradict its own minutes.

122. The person first named on a Special Committee shall act as Chairman until another is chosen by the members of the Committee; and the mover of a resolution referred to a Special Committee is usually the first named thereon.

123. Any member may excuse himself from serving on a Committee, if, at the time of his appointment, he is a member of two other Committees; but a member cannot be appointed on a Committee when absent from the Lodge.

124. A Committee cannot be discharged until all the debts contracted by it shall have been paid.

CONSTITUTION.

125. The Constitution for subordinate Lodges shall not be altered or amended unless the proposed alteration or amendment be submitted in writing, signed by five Representatives, at a regular session of the Grand Lodge, when the Grand Recording and Corresponding Scribe shall have the provision printed and furnish each Representative with a copy, and each Lodge with three copies. The proposition then being approved by the concurrent votes of two-thirds of the Representatives present at the next succeeding stated session, it shall be considered part of the Constitution, annulling and repealing all such parts as conflict therewith.

126. The Constitution of the Grand Lodge shall not be amended, unless such proposed amendments be submitted in writing at a regular session, signed by three Representatives, when the Grand Recording and Corresponding Scribe shall cause said amendments to be printed, and distribute copies thereof to each subordinate Lodge within this jurisdiction, and at the next regular session the question shall be taken on their adoption, and if approved by a vote of two-thirds of the Lodges represented entitled to vote, and the Supreme Lodge, they shall become a part of this Constitution.

5

CONTEMPT.

127. Every member is bound faithfully and punctually to attend when summoned by the Lodge, Grand Lodge, or any of their Committees or officers; and every member evading a receipt of a notice, or, after receiving notice, neglecting to attend at the time and place specified, or to continue his attendance until released, shall be reported to the Lodge, and be fined or suspended for contempt, in accordance with the laws, rules, and regulations.

DEBT.

128. Actual fraud practised by one brother upon another, either in contracting a debt or evading the payment of one already contracted, will render such brother liable to charge and punishment; but the mere neglect or refusal to pay a debt will not: if such refusal or neglect arises from any other cause than fraud, the parties must be left to the ordinary forms of law for the settlement of the dispute.

DECORUM.

129. During the reading of the minutes, communications, and other papers, and when a member is speaking, silence shall be observed in the Lodge-room.

DECORUM.

130. Any member who may misbehave himself in the meetings of the Lodge, disturb the order or harmony thereof, either by abusive, disorderly, or profane language, or may refuse obedience to the presiding officer, shall be admonished of his offence from the chair; and if he offend again, he shall be excluded from the room for the evening, and afterwards dealt with as the laws prescribe.

131. The Worthy Chancellor having taken the chair, the officers and members shall clothe themselves in regalia, and take their respective seats, and at the sound of the gavel, to be repeated by the Vice Chancellor, there shall be silence.

DEGREES.

132. A brother on whom the Page degree has legally been conferred can cause application to be made to the Lodge on the same evening for the Esquire's degree, by payment for the degree to the Financial Scribe, who must give notice to the Lodge, when open in the Knight's degree, that the brother has paid for the Esquire's degree, and desires to be raised to that degree; and when the Esquire's degree has been conferred not less than one week from the date of receiving the

DEGREES.

Page degree, he may in like manner pay for and cause application to be made for the Knight's degree; but not less than one week must elapse between the conferring of the degrees, after the charter has been closed.

133. A Lodge has no right to authorize the conferring of degrees by its officers during a recess of the Lodge, or at any time except at the stated meetings of the Lodge.

134. A Lodge having conferred degrees upon a person who was not legally entitled to them, cannot rescind its action in the case. Should the brother be of such a bad character as to be unfit to be a member of the Order, the only legal course to pursue is, to bring charges against him, and, if sustained, remove him from the Lodge in a constitutional manner.

135. A member having taken all the obligations required in a subordinate Lodge, such Lodge is not justifiable in withholding from him any part or parts of the degrees by reason of charges pending against him.

136. At balloting on an application for degrees, if all the balls deposited are white, or not more than two black, the Worthy Chancellor shall declare the applicant elected; but if there

DEGREES.

have been three BLACK BALLS deposited, the Worthy Chancellor shall declare the applicant rejected, and he shall not be entitled to renew his application until three months thereafter.

137. The least amount to be charged for the three degrees, when the charter is open, is six dollars.

138. The Grand Lodge cannot confer the degree of Past Chancellor on a member of a subordinate Lodge without the consent of said Lodge, and without a knowledge of the member's standing in the Lodge.

DISPENSATIONS.

139. Dispensations may be granted by the Grand Chancellor or his Deputy upon application from a Lodge, for the following purposes :

To propose, elect, and initiate at the same session.

To confer the three degrees at the same session.

To confer the degrees upon a person over fifty years of age.

140. It requires a fee of two dollars for a dispensation to propose, elect, and initiate a candidate on the same night. To confer more than one degree on one and the same evening, one

DISPENSATIONS.

dollar for each degree; all other dispensations, twenty-five cents each.

141. A Grand Lodge cannot grant a dispensation to initiate a person who has lost a limb.

142. It is not lawful for the Grand Chancellor to grant a dispensation to any Lodge to reopen or keep open the charter books if the membership of such Lodge is two hundred and fifty.

143. A dispensation having been asked for a certain purpose and time, and been paid for, but being received too late to be of any avail, the fee must be refunded to the party having paid the same.

DISTRICT DEPUTY GRAND CHANCELLOR.

144. The District Deputy Grand Chancellor is the representative of the Grand Chancellor in the district placed under his jurisdiction, and it shall be his duty to see that the work of the Order is performed uniformly; to install, or cause to be installed, the officers of the Lodges under his charge, and report his doings to the Grand Chancellor in time for the sessions of the Grand Lodge. He shall receive from the Grand Recording and Corresponding Scribe all dispen-

DISTRICT DEPUTY GRAND CHAN-CELLOR.

sations for new Lodges under his jurisdiction, after they may have been granted by the Grand Lodge or the Grand Officers, and, with the assistance of such Past Chancellors as he may select, open such new Lodges, deliver the dispensations, and install the officers. He shall, when visiting subordinate Lodges in his district, be provided with his commission, to be delivered to him by the Grand Chancellor on his appointment. He shall also perform such other duties as the Grand Lodge or the Grand Chancellor may, from time to time, order and direct. All necessary reasonable expenses of the District Deputy Grand Chancellor shall be paid by the Grand Lodge.

145. A District Deputy Grand Chancellor has not the power to approve By-Laws of a subordinate Lodge.

146. It is the duty of the Grand Recording and Corresponding Scribe to furnish each District Deputy Grand Chancellor with a record book, at the expense of the Grand Lodge, in which shall be recorded all official correspondence and decisions, which may be given in matters relating to the Order within the district. This book to remain in the office of the District

DISTRICT DEPUTY GRAND CHANCELLOR.

Deputy Grand Chancellors as a record for future reference, to be transferred over to each successor in office as soon as qualified.

147. The law requires a District Deputy Grand Chancellor to present a full report to the Grand Chancellor previous to each session of the Grand Lodge.

148. District Deputy Grand Chancellors are required to keep an accurate account of all dispensations issued by them, and the purpose for which they were issued, in a book furnished each District Deputy Grand Chancellor. These officers are not authorized to approve By-Laws, or amendments to the By-Laws, of any subordinate Lodge. The District Deputy Grand Chancellors must keep an accurate account of the expenses incurred, and at the end of the term, immediately after the installation of their Lodges, make a return of the full amount they have received, including all received for dispensations or other receipts, and forward the same, with their bill for expenses. No District Deputy Grand Chancellor can pay himself out of the receipts; all payments must be made on orders regularly drawn.

DONATIONS.

149. When a worthy brother is unable to pay his dues, a Lodge may grant a donation for that purpose, to keep him in good standing.

150. A Lodge receiving a dispensation to keep their charter books open for a given period, and to receive and confer all the degrees on an applicant for the sum of six dollars, it cannot evade the spirit of the law by the enactment of a resolution donating to the applicant any portion of the six dollars thus received and crediting it as dues. A violation of the law in this manner should cause a revocation of the dispensation immediately.

DUES.

151. The fiscal week by which dues must be calculated commences at the first meeting on conferring the Page's degree, and accrue weekly at the regular stated meetings of the Lodge, and may be paid at any time during the session; fractions of a week cannot be charged, nor can fractions of a week for benefits be allowed.

152. Funeral dues and fines remaining unpaid at the end of a term are counted with the weekly dues, and if the aggregate of funeral and weekly dues and fines at the end of the term amount to more than three months weekly dues, the

DUES.

brother so indebted will be in arrearage to his Lodge.

153. A brother owing three months dues on a certain meeting night, and neglecting to pay the same during that session, but coming forward to pay them on next meeting night, must, in order to appear square on the books, pay the additional week's dues.

154. Every member shall pay into the funds of the Lodge, as dues, the sum prescribed in the By-Laws, which shall in no case be at a less rate than ten cents each per week, and the amount specified for funeral tax, to commence with the date of his initiation.

155. If a member pays his weekly dues promptly, funeral tax and other fines which he may owe do not deprive him of receiving benefits, if taken sick before the end of the term, until they are charged against him as dues under the law.

156. All dues overpaid by a brother at the time of granting his card must be returned to him.

157. All dues overpaid by a brother at the time of his death must be returned to his nearest competent relative.

DUES.

158. Any amount a Lodge may owe an officer for services cannot be taken as an offset for his dues ; he is required to pay his dues regularly, the same as any other member.

ELECTIONS.

159. There shall not be an election for officers in a subordinate Lodge without a previous nomination of candidates, and sufficient time allowed to intervene for the preparation of tickets, and the majority of all the valid votes polled for the office shall be required to elect a candidate to any office; but votes polled for candidates who have not been duly nominated shall be excluded from the number.

160. When an election is held for any officer or officers in a subordinate Lodge, the presiding officer shall act as judge, and appoint two members having the Knight's degree as tellers, to assist in conducting the election in a fair and impartial manner; and when the poll has been opened, each member of good standing in the Lodge, qualified to vote, and desirous of voting, shall present his ticket to the tellers, to be deposited in the poll or box.

161. Upon an election of officers, there being more than one candidate for a particular office,

ELECTIONS.

and it being subsequently discovered that the brother elected was not in good standing, and therefore ineligible, the votes cast for him were clearly illegal, whilst neither of the opposing candidates had a majority of the votes cast, and could therefore not be elected. The election must be declared null and void and a new one ordered.

162. In order to elect a member off the floor to an office, the incumbent of which must according to the Constitution have previously served in a lower office, a dispensation must be obtained from the Grand Lodge or Grand Chancellor.

163. Votes offered by proxy shall not be received, and a register of all the votes polled must be kept.

164. Whenever the counting of the votes polled discloses a greater number than there were legally qualified members voting, (according to the list kept by the tellers,) the Worthy Chancellor shall declare the balloting at which they were received illegal and void, and direct another balloting to take place immediately.

165. In case there are two or more candidates for the same office, neither of whom having

ELECTIONS.

received a majority of all the valid votes polled for that office, another balloting shall be had, confined to the two candidates who had previously received the highest number of votes.

166. At an election for officers of the Grand Lodge by the Past Chancellors of good standing in their respective Lodges, a printed list of the qualified candidates shall be furnished by the Grand Recording and Corresponding Scribe; votes offered by proxy shall not be received, and the name of every Past Chancellor voting shall be placed on the register made by the tellers; after the poll has been closed, the tellers shall count the votes that have been received, and present them, together with their report, to the presiding officer, who shall announce the result; all the votes that have been received shall be forthwith sent, under the seal of the Lodge, attested by the signatures of the Worthy Chancellor and Recording Scribe, marked " ELECTION RETURNS," to the office of the Grand Recording and Corresponding Scribe, and a true record of the particulars of the election be made by the Recording Scribe on the minutes of the Lodge, a certified copy of which shall be furnished to the Representative of the Lodge.

EMBLEMS.

167. No member can expose any emblems of the Order, or any thing relating to the Knights of Pythias, on any sign; and any member guilty of such practices may be punished by his Lodge for so doing, either by reprimand, fine, or suspension.

168. The adoption of the regalia and other emblems designating the officers of a Lodge is not within the province of a subordinate Lodge. All such matters belong exclusively to the Supreme Lodge.

EXCUSES.

169. The By-Laws of a Lodge providing for a fine to be imposed upon absent officers unless a reasonable excuse is offered by them, it is not for the Worthy Chancellor but for the Lodge to decide whether the excuse offered shall be accepted or not.

FEES.

170. All moneys paid into the Lodge must be received by the Financial Scribe; he, the Financial Scribe, to pay over immediately such sums as he may receive to the Banker, taking his receipt therefor. Should an application for

FEES.

membership be presented, it must be handed
over to the Financial Scribe, who, after taking
possession of the fee enclosed, should give his
acknowledgment of the same on the face of the
application, and hand the application over to the
Recording Scribe to be read to the Lodge.

FINANCE COMMITTEE.

171. It shall be the duty of the Committee
on Finance and Mileage to meet at the office of
the Grand Recording and Corresponding Scribe
once in every month, at which time all bills
against the Grand Lodge shall be presented for
their approval; and it is not lawful for the
Grand Banker to pay any moneys on account of
the Grand Lodge without the approval of the
said Committee.

FINANCIAL SCRIBE.

172. The Financial Scribe shall be elected
annually, at the time prescribed by the Constitution.

173. He shall keep correct accounts between
the Lodge and its members.

174. He shall receive all moneys for the

FINANCIAL SCRIBE.

Lodge, and pay the same immediately to the Banker, and take his receipt therefor.

175. He shall furnish the Recording Scribe with the amount of receipts previous to the close of each meeting; also a list of all Past Chancellors not entitled to admission in the Grand Lodge, and of all members in arrears to the Lodge to the amount of three months dues.

176. He shall perform such other duties as are enjoined by the laws, rules, and regulations, and receive for his services such compensation as the By-Laws may prescribe.

FINES.

177. The Venerable Patriarch and assistants being duly installed in office for the performance of certain duties, *they are* liable to punishment. The Venerable Patriarch can be fined, and the assistants fined and removed.

178. If a member or an officer is fined by the Worthy Chancellor or by the Lodge for neglect of duty or breach of decorum, he is not suspended if he neglects to pay his fine, but is debarred from being installed into office, from

FINES.

taking his card, or from performing any act which requires him to be clear of the books of the Lodge; and if he is taken sick, the fine may be deducted from his benefits.

179. To fine a member upon a report made by a Committee on Charges requires the concurrence of two-thirds of the ballots cast.

180. If the By-Laws of a Lodge express the amount of fine as a penalty for neglect of duty, the Worthy Chancellor directs the Recording Scribe to note the fine as the law directs, but if it is not so expressed in the By-Laws, it requires two-thirds of the members present, voting, to fine for neglect of duty.

181. If a brother should be found guilty of an offence for which the By-Laws of the Lodge prescribe a certain punishment, the Lodge must take action on that particular penalty, and if two-thirds of the members present, voting, concur therein, he is fined, and not until then.

182. A by-law providing for the fining of subordinate members for non-attendance at stated meetings is null and void.

FLAGS.

183. The regulation flag of the Order is to be six feet long, and two feet six inches wide.

Any other sized flag must be, in width, two-thirds of the length.

Material to be silk, bunting, or muslin.

Colors, blue, yellow, and red, equal size, vertical.

184. For the Grand Lodge, a red shield with a tilting spear, and the letter "P" in the centre of the yellow.

185. For a subordinate Lodge, a red and white shield, red above, tilting spear, and letter "P" as above.

FRAUD.

186. A mere failure to keep a promise to repay borrowed money does not constitute fraud ; neither does neglect or inability to pay a debt.

FUNDS.

187. Funds paid into the treasury for the relief of the sick, the burial of the dead, the education of orphans, or other legitimate purposes, cannot be expended in pleasure excursions, picnics, or the like, they not being the legitimate purposes of a Lodge.

GOOD STANDING.

188. Every member of the Lodge shall be considered in good standing who is not disqualified, debarred, or suspended from the privileges and benefits by reason of non-payment of his dues, fines, funeral tax, or suffering from charges under the penal provisions of the laws, rules, and regulations.

GRAND LODGE.

189. The Grand Lodge shall have jurisdiction over all Lodges of Knights of Pythias within the State of Pennsylvania. It possesses the right and power of granting charters, of sus-

GRAND LODGE.

pending or taking away the same upon proper cause, of receiving and hearing all appeals, of redressing grievances and complaints arising in the Lodges under its jurisdiction, of enacting laws for its government and support, provided the same are not in violation of the laws of the Supreme Lodge.

190. It shall be composed of all Past Chancellors of good standing in subordinate Lodges in the State; but no Past Chancellor shall be permitted to speak or vote on any subject before the Grand Lodge unless he be a regularly elected Representative of a subordinate Lodge.

191. The Grand Lodge shall regulate the price of charters, dispensations, rituals, installation work, odes, and withdrawal cards. In no case shall the price of charters be less than fifteen dollars.

GRAND OFFICERS.

192. The Grand Chancellor shall preside at all sessions of the Grand Lodge, enforce order and decorum, decide all questions of order without debate, subject, however, to an appeal to the Grand Lodge by two members; appoint Grand Officers, *pro tem.*, in case of the temporary ab-

GRAND OFFICERS.

sence or disqualification of any Grand Officer;
appoint all Committees, unless otherwise ordered;
sign all orders drawn on the Grand Banker for
such sums as may be voted by the Grand Lodge,
and such other papers as may require his signature to authenticate them; exercise a general supervision over the Order in this jurisdiction. He
shall call the Vice Grand Chancellor to his chair
during the discussion of any question before the
Grand Lodge on which he may desire to speak.
He shall, at the annual session, appoint District
Deputy Grand Chancellors, and the following
Committees, to serve for the term of one year,
to wit:

A Committee on Laws and Supervision.
A Committee on Finance and Mileage.
A Committee on Appeals and Grievances.
A Committee on Returns and Credentials.
A Committee on Printing and Supplies.
A Committee of Superintendence.
A Committee on the State of the Order.

193. He shall at each stated session present
and cause to be read to the Grand Lodge his
semi-annual report. He shall visit, officially, at
least once during his term of office, accompanied
by such of his Grand Officers as he may select,
each subordinate Lodge in the district in which

GRAND OFFICERS.

he resides. All necessary reasonable expenses incurred on such visits shall be paid by this Grand Lodge.

194. The Grand Vice Chancellor is the counsellor and assistant of the Grand Chancellor. In the absence of the Grand Chancellor he shall preside over the Grand Lodge. In case of the removal, death, resignation, or inability of the Grand Chancellor, the powers of said office shall devolve on the Grand Vice Chancellor for the time being.

195. The Grand Recording and Corresponding Scribe shall keep a just and true record of all the proceedings of the Grand Lodge at each session, and transmit semi-annually to each subordinate Lodge two copies thereof—one for the Representative, and the other for the use of the Lodge.

196. He shall preserve the archives, have charge of the seal, books, papers, and other properties of the Grand Lodge, and deliver the same to his successor when required so to do by the Grand Lodge.

197. He shall prepare all charters and dispensations for subordinate Lodges.

GRAND OFFICERS.

198. He shall notify officially all subordinate Lodges within the State of all meetings of the Grand Lodge.

199. He shall carry on the necessary correspondence of the Grand Lodge.

200. He shall keep a register containing a list of all charters granted to subordinate Lodges, of all Past Chancellors and Representatives entitled to seats in the Grand Lodge, and of all rejected candidates and suspended members.

201. He shall attest all official papers and documents.

202. He shall receive all moneys due to the Grand Lodge, and pay them over immediately to the Grand Banker, taking his receipt therefor, and keep an exact and true account of the same; draw all orders on the Grand Banker for such moneys as may be voted by the Grand Lodge, and attest the same; report in writing at the annual session, and at other times when so required by the Grand Lodge, the condition of the funds of the Grand Lodge, and of the accounts of the subordinate Lodges; and deliver the books to the Finance Committee whenever they may demand them.

GRAND OFFICERS.

203. He shall have power to provide himself, at the expense of the Grand Lodge, with such books, papers, and stationery, as are necessary for the fulfilment of his duties.

204. He shall keep in his office a copy of the seal of each subordinate Lodge in his jurisdiction.

205. He shall perform such other duties as are required by the laws and regulations of the Order, and as the Grand Lodge may from time to time direct.

206. He shall give security in such sum as the Grand Lodge may determine, and receive for the faithful performance of his duties such salary as the By-Laws may prescribe.

207. He shall be furnished with an office, have regular hours for the transaction of official business, and give notice to the subordinate Lodges of the time at which he will so attend.

208. He shall at each annual session present to the Grand Lodge a report of the general condition of the Order.

209. The following blanks will be furnished by the Grand Recording and Corresponding Scribe :

GRAND OFFICERS.

Blank semi-annual returns.

Blank Past Chancellors' certificates.

Blank Representatives' certificates.

Blank dispensations.

Blank District Deputy Grand Chancellors' commissions.

Blank form of applications for charter.

210. The Grand Banker shall receive all funds for the use of the Grand Lodge from the Grand Recording and Corresponding Scribe, giving to him a receipt for the same; pay all orders drawn on him by the Grand Chancellor, properly attested; keep the accounts in a proper manner, exhibiting the sources and amounts of receipts, and the purposes and amounts of disbursements; and give a statement in writing thereof at the stated session, or whenever required to do so by the Grand Lodge. At the expiration of his term of office, he shall deliver all books, papers, and moneys (belonging to the Grand Lodge and in his possession) to his successor. Before entering upon the duties of his office, he shall give such security for the faithful performance of his trust as the Grand Lodge may deem satisfactory, and deliver the books to the Finance Committee for examination whenever they may demand them.

GRAND OFFICERS.

211. The Grand Guide shall assist in the ceremonies of the Grand Lodge, and in preserving order therein; examine and conduct new members and Representatives in the Grand Lodge; and execute the commands of the Grand Chancellor.

212. The Grand Inner Steward shall have charge of the inner door; he shall see that all members of the Grand Lodge are clothed in appropriate regalia before entering the Lodge-room.

213. The Grand Outer Steward shall have charge of the outer door; allow no person to enter the ante-room without the password, unless ordered so to do by the Grand Chancellor; and be responsible for the safe-keeping of all the regalias, jewels, and other property of the Grand Lodge while that body is in session. For the faithful performance of his duties, he shall receive such sum as the By-Laws may prescribe.

214. The Grand Representatives shall attend the sessions of the Supreme Lodge of the Knights of Pythias, and therein faithfully represent the views, interests, and special instructions directed by a vote of the Grand Lodge; make a report in writing of their acts and

GRAND OFFICERS.

doings, and of such matters and transactions of the Supreme Lodge as affect the Grand Lodge and the well-being of the Order in general, at the next succeeding session; and do and perform such other duties appertaining to their official stations as are enjoined by the laws, rules, and regulations.

GUIDE.

215. The Guide shall be elected semi-annually, at the last stated meetings of the term.

216. He shall have charge of the properties of the Lodge, and be held responsible for their safe-keeping.

217. He shall perform such duties as are required by the work of the Order and enjoined by the laws, rules, and regulations.

INCORPORATION.

218. No subordinate Lodge has the right to ask for or receive any act of incorporation, whether from the Courts, Legislature, or any source whatever. Such an act would be insubordination, and cause the Grand Lodge to forfeit the charter of such Lodge.

INITIATION.

219. The initiation of a person, after having been regularly elected, cannot be prevented by objections raised after his election, unless the objections are sustained by the Lodge.

INNER STEWARD.

220. The Inner Steward shall be elected semi-annually, at the last stated meetings of the term.

221. He shall perform such duties as are required by the work of the Order and enjoined by the laws, rules, and regulations.

INSTALLATION.

222. The accounts of the term must be settled and audited, the semi-annual report made out, and the per capita tax due the Grand Lodge paid to the installing officers before the installation of the officers of a subordinate Lodge can take place.

223. If an officer be not legally nominated and elected, the act of installation becomes void.

224. Any legal expense incurred by the installing officer, on the occasion of installation of officers in a subordinate Lodge, are paid by the Grand Lodge.

INSTALLATION.

225. Officers of the Lodge legally elected (if qualified) shall be installed at the first stated meeting in the ensuing term. Any officer who has been duly elected failing to present himself for installation (unless prevented by sickness or some other unavoidable occurrence) may have the office to which he has been elected declared vacant by the installing officer, and another election be ordered forthwith to fill the vacancy.

INSTITUTION OF NEW LODGES.

226. No Lodge can be instituted unless the applicants have possession or control of the paraphernalia necessary for the work of the Order.

227. At the institution of a new Lodge, the applicants must pay the necessary travelling expenses of the installing officers.

228. At the institution of a new Lodge, the installing officers have no right to initiate strangers previous to institution, except in cases where the applicants for charter are not Knights.

LEGISLATION.

229. It is not the prerogative of any Grand Officer, either elective or appointed, to set aside during the recess any legislation of the Grand Lodge.

LOANS.

230. A Lodge is not bound to refund donations or loans made to a member by a sister Lodge; the matter rests altogether with the Lodge.

MAIMED.

231. Persons so maimed as to be unable to perform the work of the Order are not eligible to membership. A dispensation can be granted to persons who have lost an eye or finger, as it does not prevent them performing the work.

MEETINGS.

232. The stated meetings of a subordinate Lodge shall be held every week, at the place and on the day appointed with the approval of the Grand Lodge, and shall not be changed without such approval; the hour of meeting to be prescribed in the By-Laws.

233. When a meeting of the Lodge has been closed, it shall not be reopened except with unanimous consent; and if any member has left the room subsequent to the closing, it shall not be reopened.

MEMBERSHIP.

234. A Lodge cannot initiate into the mysteries of the Order any person who is not a

MEMBERSHIP.

white male, over twenty-one and under fifty years of age, of good moral character, with all his parts, healthy, sound, and free from any mental or bodily infirmity, able and competent to earn the means necessary for the support of himself and family, and a believer in the Supreme Creator and Preserver of the universe, nor for a less sum than the amount prescribed.

235. Each application for membership shall be accompanied with not less than $5, (except when from a brother of the Order with his withdrawal card, not less than $2.50,) be signed by the applicant, state his age, occupation, and residence, with the recommendation of two Knights, members of good standing in the Lodge; which application shall be read at a stated meeting, entered on the record, and referred to a Committee of three members, Knights, (neither of whom shall have recommended the applicant,) to make the necessary investigations, and report as to the character and other qualifications of the applicant for membership at the next stated meeting.

236. Every applicant for membership reported upon by the Committee shall be balloted for separately, at a stated meeting; and all the

MEMBERSHIP.

balls deposited being white, or not more than one black, the Worthy Chancellor shall declare the applicant elected. Should two or more black balls appear against a candidate, the ballot shall be renewed immediately; but if there have been two or more deposited on the second ballot, he shall be declared rejected; and no other balloting for the same applicant shall take place in any Lodge of the Order within the jurisdiction until the expiration of six months thereafter, when another application for membership may be received from the rejected applicant.

237. It is legal to receive applications for membership on the night of closing the charter, at charter rates, and to ballot for them on the next stated meeting of the Lodge.

238. Every applicant elected to membership, failing to present himself for initiation or admission within four stated meetings of the Lodge after being notified of his election, (unless prevented by sickness or some other unavoidable occurrence,) shall forfeit the amount that has been paid by him to the Lodge.

239. Members of any defunct Lodge who were in good standing at the time of dissolution

MEMBERSHIP.

may be admitted into any other Lodge, after having applied to and received from the Grand Lodge a card signed by the Grand Chancellor, and countersigned by the Grand Recording and Corresponding Scribe, with the seal of the Grand Lodge attached. The application for such card must be accompanied by the fee of $2, the card to hold good twelve months.

240. A member of the Order, notified to appear before a Committee, or to produce books, documents, papers, or other articles in his possession or under his control, shall attend at the time and place specified, and continue his attendance until dismissed, or subject himself to a charge for contempt, and be fined or suspended, as may be determined on complaint of the Committee.

241. An alien may make application for membership.

242. A verbal application for membership cannot be received by any Lodge.

243. A person wishing to become a member of a Lodge remote from his place of residence, the Lodge to which he makes application must give immediate notice to the Lodge or Lodges in the vicinity of the applicant's residence; if, at

MEMBERSHIP.

the expiration of two weeks from the date of such notice, no reply is received, a Committee may then be appointed to proceed in regular form. If, however, a reply is received from the Lodge or Lodges notified, setting forth any objections as to the personal character, health, or other qualifications of the applicant, then the Lodge having entertained the proposition shall appoint a Committee, who shall investigate the objections so made, giving due notice thereof to the objecting Lodge, and report upon the facts in the case. If these objections, after careful investigation, be not sustained, the applicant may be elected and initiated as before provided.

244. An application for membership cannot be withdrawn when a part of the Committee of Investigation into the fitness of the candidate report favorably and the remainder unfavorably upon such application. In such cases a ballot must be had.

245. A person who is unable to sign his own petition is ineligible to membership in this Order.

246. A brother of the Order, wishing to join a Lodge on card, must, in addition to his card, present an application duly signed by

MEMBERSHIP.

him, and indorsed by two members of the
Knight's degree.

MILEAGE.

247. No Representative is entitled to mileage
unless he be present at one of the regular roll-
calls on the first or second day of the session.

MINUTES.

248. The minutes should be a *correct record
of the proceedings* of the Lodge at its sessions,
and when read by the Recording Scribe, they
can only be objected to on the ground of incor-
rectness. The legality or illegality of the proceedings is a matter over which the Recording
Scribe has no control. He must make up his
record, and the Lodge must approve if that is
correctly kept.

249. The question of the legality or uncon-
stitutionality of the business of the Lodge cannot
be considered when the question before the
Lodge is upon the approval of the minutes, but
must be brought up under the head of new
business.

MOTIONS.

250. A motion to adjourn is always in order
after the regular Lodge business is gone through,

MOTIONS.

which motion shall be decided without debate;
but if decided in the affirmative, it is no adjournment until the Lodge is closed in due form.

251. A motion to lie on the table shall be
decided without debate.

252. A motion having been regularly made,
the Worthy Chancellor may, if he deem proper,
silently second it by saying "it has been moved
and seconded," without waiting for the motion
to be formally seconded.

NAME.

253. The name or initials of the Order cannot be used for any other purpose than the
business of the Order.

254. No new Lodge shall be allowed to be
named after any person living at the time of its
institution.

NOMINATIONS.

255. Nominations for candidates for the
several elective offices in a subordinate Lodge
shall be made at the two stated meetings of the
Lodge immediately preceding the election, and
any candidate nominated on the day or night of
election shall be considered ineligible, unless

NOMINATION.

some unforeseen circumstance renders it necessary; the presiding officer shall not close the nominations until every member present has had an opportunity to be heard, nor shall a qualified member, duly nominated, be excluded from the list of nominees because he is not present.

NOMINEES.

256. It is the duty of the Grand Recording and Corresponding Scribe to notify all brothers nominated for offices in the Grand Lodge of such nomination within thirty days thereafter, omitting the names of all who have not signified their acceptance by the 1st of October ensuing.

OFFICERS.

257. A brother having served a majority of nights in an office and subsequently resigned his position, is not qualified to fill a higher office if elected thereto by his Lodge.

258. To be advanced, an officer must be present and serve in his official position a majority of the nights in a term, unless prevented by sickness or some unavoidable occurrence satisfactory to the Lodge, and unless elected to fill a vacancy.

259. To remove an officer for non-attendance

8

OFFICERS.

or gross neglect of duty, he should be notified (by a notice properly attested) to appear at a regular stated session (not less than one week thereafter) and show cause why his office should not be vacated. Should he not appear at the time stated, or should he fail to present a constitutional excuse, the Lodge may, by a two-thirds vote, declare him removed from office, and proceed to fill the vacancy.

OUTER STEWARD.

260. The Outer Steward shall be elected annually, at the time prescribed by law.

261. He shall perform such duties as are required by the work of the Order and enjoined by the laws, rules, and regulations; and receive for his services such compensation as the By-Laws may prescribe.

PAST CHANCELLOR.

262. The Recording Scribe, Financial Scribe, Banker, and Outer Steward, having served to the end of the term from institution of the Lodge without compensation, at installation of their successors for second term become Past Chancellors.

263. A Past Chancellor, whether by dispen-

PAST CHANCELLOR.

sation or otherwise, may be elected to the office of Worthy Chancellor, and is also qualified to hold the office of Representative at the same time.

264. If a Past Chancellor presents himself for admission to the Grand Lodge and his certificate is not on file in the office of the Grand Recording Scribe, the report of his Lodge cannot be taken as *evidence* that he is a Past Chancellor and entitle him to admission. The law expressly states that *previous* to being admitted as a member of the Grand Lodge, he must present his certificate under seal of his Lodge, attested by the Worthy Chancellor and Recording Scribe.

PENALTIES.

265. There is no such penalty as "expulsion" in the Order.

266. A member having been found guilty of a charge, the law prescribing that he may be either fined, removed from office, or suspended, and a vote having been taken upon one or both of the first two penalties, and decided in the negative, the third or last penalty is thereby not imposed: a ballot must be taken thereon in proper form, for a refusal on the part of a

PENALTIES.

Lodge to impose the lesser penalties does not, of necessity, inflict the greater.

267. Whilst it is in the province of a Lodge to give instructions to its officers to perform duties which are of a benefit to the Lodge, yet it has no right to inflict penalties by a simple resolution for a violation of duties prescribed by that resolution, and originated in it. This should be engrafted in a by-law.

PETITIONS.

268. All Lodges under this jurisdiction that may circulate, among their sister Lodges, any petition for aid for distressed members or their families, shall have printed upon such petition a correct statement of the amount of the available funds of the Lodge, otherwise the Grand Chancellor must refuse to sanction the circulation.

269. All communications, petitions, and memorials shall be presented through a member of the Lodge, or by the presiding officer, and a brief statement of their contents shall be entered on the minutes.

POSTAGE.

270. Any expense for postage or expressage in transmitting the benefits or communications

POSTAGE.

to a member located at a distance from the Lodge must be defrayed by such member.

PRESIDING OFFICER.

271. The Vice Chancellor or Past Chancellor who may occupy the chair of the Worthy Chancellor in the absence of the Worthy Chancellor is invested for the time being with all the power and authority of that officer.

272. In the absence of both the Worthy Chancellor and Vice Chancellor, the senior Past Chancellor present shall take the chair, but if no Past Chancellor be present, any member of good standing, having the Knight's degree, may be chosen to preside by the majority of the members present.

PROBATION.

273. It is a constitutional requirement of every Lodge in this jurisdiction to set forth in their By-Laws a probationary period, or, in other words, a certain time to expire previous to members of the Knight's degree becoming beneficial; this is done in order to create a fund to place the Lodge upon a firm and solid basis; and a member becoming sick or disabled pending the time of probation fixed in the By-Laws

PROBATION.

would not be entitled to weekly benefits until the
expiration of the time as set forth in the By-
Laws; yet any brother if taken sick or disabled
after having been initiated into the Order he
becomes a charity member, subject (if in distressed circumstances) to such donations of
charity as the Lodge may see fit to donate: *Provided,* He is not disqualified as set forth in the
laws of the Order; *and provided always,* That
his disability is not of a permanent character.
This exempts all of a permanent character, and
includes those of a temporary or local character.
This is intended to prevent members from claiming benefits where other men similarly afflicted
continue plying at their vocations.

PROCESSIONS.

274. A Lodge shall not make a public dis-
play, (except on the occasion of a funeral,)
without permission from the Grand Lodge, or,
during the recess, from the Grand Chancellor;
and when in procession of any kind, it shall be
under the guidance of its marshals, and proceed
according to the laws, rules, and regulations.

PYTHIAN PERIOD.

275. The "Pythian Period" dates back,
and commences on the 19th day of February,

PYTHIAN PERIOD.

1864; and each and every year thereafter, and to come, shall succeed in regular numerical order, commencing on the 19th day of February of each year.

QUESTION.

276. Any member may call for a division of the question when the sense will admit of it; but a motion to strike out and insert shall be indivisible, except at the option of the mover.

277. A question shall not be subject to debate until it has been seconded and stated from the chair; and it shall be reduced to writing at the request of any member.

278. When a question is before the Lodge, no motion shall be in order except to adjourn, for the previous question, to postpone indefinitely, to postpone for a certain time, to divide, to commit, or to amend; which motions shall severally have precedence in the order herein arranged.

279. On the call of seven members, debate shall cease and a vote be taken on the motion or question under debate.

280. On the call of seven members, a majority of the Lodge may demand the previous question, which shall always be in this form—

QUESTION.

"Shall the main question be put?"—and until it is decided, shall preclude all amendments and all further debate.

281. When a question is postponed indefinitely, it shall not be acted on during that or the next succeeding stated meeting; if in the Grand Lodge, it may be acted on at the next succeeding session.

QUORUM.

282. It requires seven Knights to constitute a quorum.

READMISSION.

283. In any case when a charter may be refused, the petitioners are entitled, if Knights, to readmission into their several Lodges upon payment of dues from the date of their respective cards.

RECESS.

234. A recess cannot be declared while the paraphernalia is exposed.

RECONSIDER.

285. A motion to reconsider must be made at the same meeting at which it was adopted,

RECONSIDER.

and by a member who voted with the majority
in the first instance.

286. A by-law passed by the constitutional
two-thirds of the legal votes present cannot be
reconsidered by a majority vote, though it may
not have been sent up for approval. The same
method of repealing the law as was pursued in
passing it must be adhered to, to legally annul
the same.

RECORDING SCRIBE.

287. The Recording Scribe shall be elected
annually at the time prescribed by law.

288. He shall keep an accurate record of all
proceedings of the Lodge.

289. He shall make out the report of the
work and business of the Lodge for the Grand
Lodge, and other documents and notices.

290. He shall notify the Grand Recording
and Corresponding Scribe of all rejections of
candidates, and of suspensions (except for non-
payment of dues) and reinstatements of members.

291. He shall attest all bills or drafts on the
Banker.

292. He shall have charge of the corre-
pondence, records, and seal of the Lodge.

RECORDING SCRIBE.

293. He shall perform such other duties as are enjoined by the laws, rules, and regulations of the Order; and receive for his compensation such sum as the By-Laws may prescribe.

REFUND.

294. A member reported to his Lodge as being sick, the Lodge paying him benefits, but subsequently discover that he was in arrears at the time he was reported, cannot be compelled to refund the amount paid to him; this being a voluntary act on the part of the Lodge, it must bear the loss.

295. Dues paid in advance by members withdrawing by card, or by deceased members, must be refunded by the Lodge to the proper parties.

REGALIA.

296. It is the duty of the officers to be clothed in the regalia of the office they hold, and they must occupy their chair or station in the Lodge in order to participate in the proceedings thereof; and the Worthy Chancellor is not required to recognize any officer unless properly clothed, and at his proper station.

297. A Past Chancellor occupying a subor-

REGALIA.

dinate office in a Lodge must wear the regalia belonging to such office.

298. The working regalia shall be as follows: For Pages, a blue collar; for Esquires, yellow collar; for Knights, a red collar; for Venerable Patriarch, a black velvet collar, with silver fringe one and a half inches long, and silver lace border on inner edge half inch wide, and an open Bible, embroidered in silver on the left side; for Worthy Chancellor, a collar of scarlet velvet, trimmed in the same manner as the Venerable Patriarch's, with crossed gavels on the left side; for Vice Chancellor, the same as the Worthy Chancellor's, with single gavel; for Recording Scribe, the same as the Vice Chancellor's, with crossed pens, omitting the fringe; for Financial Scribe, the same as the Recording Scribe's, with pen and key crossed; for Banker, the same as the Financial Scribe's, with crossed keys; for Guide, the same as the Banker's, with crossed staffs; for Inner Steward, the same as the Guide's, with crossed swords; for Outer Steward, the same as the Inner Steward's, with single sword; for Past Chancellor, scarlet velvet collar, trimmed with gold fringe.

299. Representatives to the Grand Lodge wear scarlet velvet collars, trimmed with gold

REGALIA.

fringe, and the number of the Lodge which they represent embroidered thereon.

300. The Venerable Grand Patriarch wears a black velvet collar with gold fringe; and the rest of the Grand Officers, scarlet velvet collars, with same fringe, each officer's collar having embroidered thereon (in gold) the insignia of office.

301. Representatives to the Supreme Lodge wear black velvet collars, trimmed with gold fringe, and the letters S. R. (embroidered in gold) on the collar.

302. Past Grand Chancellors wear black velvet collars, trimmed with gold fringe, and the letters P. G. C. embroidered thereon.

303. For District Deputy Grand Chancellor, the working regalia shall be a red velvet collar, trimmed with gold fringe, and the letters D. G. C. embroidered thereon in gold.

REINSTATEMENTS.

304. The arrearages due by a member who has been suspended for non-payment of dues, and who applies for reinstatement, are simply the amount due at the time of his suspension. Each Lodge can, however, regulate by its own By-

REINSTATEMENTS.

Laws what additional amount shall be charged or penalty imposed upon his reinstatement.

305. In balloting on the report of a Committee upon the application of a suspended member (except for suspension for non-payment of dues) to be restored to membership before the term of suspension has expired, two-thirds of the votes cast are necessary to reinstate, provided permission of the Grand Lodge is first obtained.

306. After a member has been elected for reinstatement, it is not necessary for him to be introduced to the Lodge; he is considered reinstated by merely liquidating the amount prescribed by the By-Laws.

REJECTIONS.

307. Candidates for membership being rejected in a certain Lodge, cannot become charter members or apply for initiation in another Lodge before the expiration of six months.

308. When an applicant for membership has been rejected, notice of his rejection must be immediately sent by the Recording Scribe to the office of the Grand Recording and Corresponding Scribe, and the amount accompanying his application be refunded

RELATIVE.

309. The term "competent relative" is defined as follows:

1. The wife, if competent, not being mentally deranged or otherwise unfitted to take charge of and make proper disposition of the fund. (There being no wife:)

2. The oldest adult male or female child. (There being no adult children:)

3. The minor children, the Worthy Chancellor acting for them. (There being no children:)

4. The father. (There being no father:)

5. The mother. (There being no mother:)

6. The brothers and sisters.

RELIEF COMMITTEE.

310. It is the duty of the Relief Committee to officially inform a brother who becomes sick, and who is not entitled to benefits, that he is not entitled, stating the cause, in order that he may, should he consider himself aggrieved by the action of the Lodge, proceed without delay to have his case investigated.

REMOVALS.

311. Any officer may be removed for inattention to the duties of his station, or conduct unbecoming his standing in the Order; and va-

REMOVALS.

cancies occurring by reason of death, resignation, or otherwise, shall be filled in the manner of the original selection, to serve for the remainder of the term only: the officer so serving shall be entitled to the full honors of the term. Every officer against whom charges are preferred shall have a fair and impartial trial in accordance with the laws, rules, and regulations of the Order, but he shall officiate until the charges have been settled, unless otherwise ordered by the Lodge.

312. To remove an officer requires the concurrence of two-thirds of the ballots cast.

REPORT, (Semi-Annual.)

313. The Grand Recording and Corresponding Scribe shall furnish each subordinate Lodge of this jurisdiction with two blank copies of the semi-annual report, one of which is to be filled out and marked *original*, and forwarded to the Grand Recording and Corresponding Scribe, and the other to be filled out in like manner, and marked *duplicate*, and filed in the archives of the Lodge.

REPRESENTATIVE.

314. Representatives to the Grand Lodge must be Past Chancellors in good standing, and

REPRESENTATIVE.

shall be elected annually by the members of the subordinate Lodges under its jurisdiction.

315. A Worthy Chancellor (unless previously a Past Chancellor) cannot be elected Representative to the Grand Lodge.

316. A Representative is not entitled to wear his badge of office in his subordinate Lodge.

317. Fines, if imposed upon Representatives for absence from the session of the Grand Lodge without leave, must be deducted from their mileage.

318. A Past Chancellor elected by his Lodge as its Representative, but has never been admitted to the Grand Lodge, and whose certificate of Past Chancellor is not on file in the office of the Grand Recording and Corresponding Scribe, cannot be admitted on his certificate as Representative; he must produce both.

319. In all contests or protests as to the legality of the election of Representatives to the Grand Lodge, the members of the Order so contesting or protesting must in the first instance do so in their subordinate Lodges; failing to receive justice therein, or being aggrieved at the decision of their Lodge, the right of appeal to

REPRESENTATIVE.

the Grand Lodge should then be exercised within the constitutional period.

320. A Representative shall receive the instructions of the Lodge, and faithfully represent its interests in the Grand Lodge.

RESCIND.

321. To rescind a resolution passed at a previous session requires a two-thirds vote.

RESIGNATION.

322. Any officer has the right to offer his resignation to the Lodge of any office to which he has been elected. The Lodge also has the right to accept the resignation of any elective officer on the night upon which it is offered, unless the By-Laws of the Lodge otherwise order.

323. A Lodge may accept the resignation of a member of Committee on Charges, and the vacancy created thereby must be filled in the manner of original selection of the Committee.

324. A Lodge cannot, by any act, sever the connection of a member of the Order *with* the Order. A member who is clear upon the books, and under no charges under the penal laws of the Order, must, on application, have a with-

RESIGNATION.

drawal card granted him, which severs his connection with the Lodge, whether the card be taken or not; but a Lodge cannot receive a resignation from the Order.

RESOLUTION.

325. The mover of a resolution has not the right to construe the same, or determine its meaning and intention.

RESTORATION.

326. When the Lodge has indefinitely suspended a member, (except for non-payment of dues,) he shall not be restored to membership in the same or any other Lodge, except by permission from the Grand Lodge.

327. All funds and effects received by the Grand Lodge from a dissolved or suspended Lodge shall be restored in the event of it being reinstated, which reinstatement may be done by a majority vote of the Grand Lodge, at a stated or special session.

RETIRING.

328. A member of the Grand Lodge cannot leave the room during the reading of any document or the pending of any question before the Chair.

RETIRING.

329. During the session of a Lodge or a recess, a brother is not required to address the Chair on retiring to the ante-room; but the Worthy Chancellor must first order the outer door to be secured so that none can depart from the jurisdiction of the Lodge and its officers.

RETURNS.

330. At the close of every term, the Lodge shall report to the Grand Lodge the number of initiations, names of brothers admitted by card, suspended, and the cause thereof, rejected or deceased; a list of all Past Chancellors not entitled to the privileges and benefits; all brothers and widowed families relieved, brothers buried, with the amount of money appropriated for each of these purposes; the number of orphans being educated, designating the schools to which they are sent, the amount paid for the same; the amount of receipts, specifying what fund; the amount of contingent expenses, and tax due the Grand Lodge; the total amount on hand, separating the general and widows' and orphans' fund; the amount invested; and the result of the election for officers, according to the form furnished by the Grand Lodge; which report shall be properly attested, and the order for the tax

RETURNS.

be drawn and delivered to the installing officer previous to installation.

331. A sitting Worthy Chancellor has not the right to sign a report returning himself as a Past Chancellor, he not having previously passed the Worthy Chancellor's chair. The return is to be made of the proceedings of the term then expiring, and must be signed by the officers in the capacity they then fill.

332. It is the duty of the Grand Scribe to notify every Lodge which fails to send its returns and tax within fifteen days after the proper time for installation of officers.

333. The semi-annual reports require each Lodge to report the number of Pages, Esquires, and Knights in good standing, and the number who are not in good standing, and the number of Past Chancellors in good standing, and the number not in good standing. A Page, Esquire, Knight, or Past Chancellor who is in arrears for three months dues or more is not in good standing, and must be returned accordingly.

REVOKE.

334. The Grand Chancellor has not the power to revoke the business of a subordinate Lodge between its sessions.

SALARY.

335. A Lodge cannot raise or lower the salary of officers pending the term for which said officers were elected.

SEAL.

336. Each Lodge must have an official seal with appropriate devices, which shall be affixed to withdrawal cards, certificates, and other official documents and papers issued by and under authority of the Lodge, an impression of which shall be deposited in the office of the Grand Recording and Corresponding Scribe.

337. It is not legal for a subordinate Lodge to adopt a seal on the face of which any part of the secret work is exposed.

338. The seal of a Lodge cannot be used except on official documents of the Lodge.

S. A. P. W.

339. A member in good standing, residing at a distance from his Lodge, or travelling, is entitled to the S. A. P. W.; and it is the duty of the Worthy Chancellor of the Lodge to which the brother belongs, upon proper application being made, to furnish the brother with a certificate directed to the nearest Lodge to his resi-

S. A. P. W.

dence or abode, requesting them, on proper examination, to impart the S. A. P. W. The Worthy Chancellor is alone authorized to communicate the term P. W. or cause it to be communicated to members.

SPEAK.

340. It is not legal for a Lodge to pass a law preventing a brother from speaking or voting on the night of his admission as a Knight.

341. A member shall not be permitted to speak or vote unless clothed in regalia suitable for his rank and station in the Lodge.

342. Each member speaking shall stand and respectfully address the Chair, confine himself to the question under debate, and avoid all personalities, indecorous or sarcastic language.

343. A member shall not be interrupted while speaking, except to call him to order for words spoken, or for the purpose of explanation.

344. If a member while speaking be called to order, he shall, at the request of the Chair, take his seat until the question of order is determined, when, if permitted, he may proceed again.

SPEAK.

345. A member shall not speak more than once on the same subject or question, until all who wish to speak may have had an opportunity to do so, nor more than twice without permission from the Chair; and every member speaking shall designate the officer or member spoken of by his proper rank or title, according to his standing in the Order.

STATE LINES.

346. Lodges in the State of Pennsylvania have no right to initiate persons residing in a sister jurisdiction. State lines must be respected.

347. If a person residing on the borders of this State is desirous of connecting himself with a Lodge under the jurisdiction of an adjoining State, said Lodge being nearest his place of residence, he may, with the consent of the Grand Chancellor, make application to a Lodge in an adjoining jurisdiction; the consent of the Grand Chancellor must accompany the application.

SUMMONS.

348. Any member of the Order summoned as a witness, or to produce such books or papers as may be required, neglecting or refusing to

SUMMONS.

obey such summons, may be fined or suspended at the option of the Lodge to which such refractory member may belong.

SUSPENSIONS.

349. When a suspended member of a subordinate Lodge is restored to membership therein by a mandate of the Grand Lodge, he is required to pay all dues accruing during the time of suspension.

350. A member being over twelve months in arrears for dues, the Financial Scribe must report the fact in open Lodge that he owes for twelve months dues or more, and is liable to suspension. One week thereafter the Worthy Chancellor may declare him suspended, unless he pays or causes to be paid a sum sufficient to reduce the amount below twelve months dues. No vote of the Lodge is required.

351. A member suspended for a definite period, under the penal laws of our Order, must pay his dues during such suspension, and all moneys sent by him to the Lodge must be placed to his credit, and at the expiration of the term of suspension he is entitled to all his rights and privileges in the Lodge and the Order, without any action of the Lodge; yet, pending

SUSPENSIONS.

his suspension from the Lodge, should he commit the same offence or other offences against the laws of the Lodge or the Order, he is liable to have charges preferred against him in the Lodge at the expiration of the term of suspension, or the Lodge can ask of the Grand Chancellor a dispensation to revoke the term of suspension, which, if granted, the Lodge can, by a two-thirds vote of the members present concurring, revoke the term of suspension, and immediately prefer charges against him, and if found guilty, after due trial, punish.

352. Suspension for an indefinite period is prohibited.

353. The Worthy Chancellor has not the right to suspend an officer under any consideration.

354. To suspend a member for a definite period requires two-thirds of the ballots cast.

355. When a Lodge is suspended or dissolved, the Worthy Chancellor, or, if there is none, its senior officer, shall deliver up the charter or dispensation, books, jewels, funds, emblems, regalia, and other property and effects to the Grand Chancellor or his deputy; and any officer or member, having any of the said prop-

10

SUSPENSIONS.

erty or effects, refusing to surrender the same, may be forever excluded from membership in the Order, even though his Lodge should be reinstated.

356. A suspended member is virtually deprived of all the rights and privileges in the Lodge and the Order ; it is therefore illegal to insert the name of such suspended member on the printed roll of members which may be attached to the By-Laws.

TAX.

357. The per capita tax must be paid on all members who have not been formally suspended from the Lodge on or before the last meeting in each term.

358. Subordinate Lodges shall pay to the Grand Lodge semi-annually, as dues, ten cents per capita tax for every member on the roll.

TERM.

359. A term is six months, terminating at the election of officers; when, if the fines or funeral tax are not paid on either of the above nights specified, they are to be charged as dues

TESTIMONY.

360. During the trial of charges it is perfectly legal for the Committee or Lodge to receive testimony from persons not members of the Order, always, however, with discrimination as to the manner of taking it, and the weight to be given to it.

TRUSTEES OF GRAND LODGE.

361. The Trustees shall have the charge and general supervision of the funds, investments, and other property belonging to the Grand Lodge, in order that they may look after its material interests and welfare; receive and hold the bonds and securities of such Grand Officers as are required to give them for the faithful discharge of their official duties; invest in such loans, stocks, or other securities as the Grand Lodge may direct, all money ordered to be drawn from the Grand Banker for that purpose, and deposit the securities received with the Grand Recording and Corresponding Scribe, to be placed in possession of the Grand Banker for safe-keeping; call in, sell, and realize all such loans, stocks, and other investments whenever the Grand Lodge shall order the same to be done; collect all the interest, dividends, rents, and other money arising or accruing from any and all the investments belonging to the Grand

TRUSTEES OF GRAND LODGE.

Lodge; pay all money collected by them to the Grand Recording and Corresponding Scribe; and report their transactions in writing to the Grand Lodge at the earliest practicable opportunity thereafter.

TRUSTEES OF SUBORDINATE LODGE.

362. There shall be three Trustees of a subordinate Lodge, one of whom shall be elected to serve for the term of eighteen months at the last stated meeting of the term, in such manner as to have two remaining over at each election.

363. The Trustees shall be charged with the general supervision and care of the funds, investments, and other Lodge property, in order that they may look after its material interests and welfare; invest in such loans, stocks, or other securities as the Lodge may direct, all money ordered to be drawn from the Banker for the purpose, and deposit the vouchers with the Financial Scribe to be placed in possession of the Banker for safe-keeping; call in, sell, and realize all such loans, stocks, and other investments whenever the Lodge may order the same to be done; collect all the interest, dividends, rents, and other money arising or accruing from any and all the investments belonging to the

TRUSTEES OF SUBORDINATE LODGE.

Lodge; pay the money collected by them to the Financial Scribe; and report their transactions to the Lodge at the next stated meeting succeeding the election for officers at the close of every term, and make an inventory of all properties of the Lodge.

364. The Worthy Chancellor, Vice Chancellor, Recording Scribe, Financial Scribe, and Banker are not eligible to serve as Trustee of the Lodge; being the executive and financial officers of the Lodge, their acts may be subject to examination, and it would not be right or proper for either of them to examine and pass upon their own official doings.

UNIFORM.
Full Gala and Inspection Dress.

365. Coat, pants, sword, belt, baldric, cloak, gorget, gauntlet cuffs, gloves, helmet and oriflamme, (with fatigue cap, covered, hung to belt.)

Ordinary Parade Dress.

366. Coat, pants, sword, belt, baldric, gauntlet cuffs, gloves, helmet and oriflamme, (with fatigue cap, covered, suspended from sword belt.)

Fatigue Dress.

367. Coat, pants, sword, belt, fatigue cap, (uncovered,) and white gloves.

ORDINARY PARADE DRESS.

UNIFORM.

Coat.

368. Black cloth, cut military style, single-breasted, standing collar, (with a half roll to the sixth button from the bottom,) nine buttons in front, two behind, length to knee, side edges plain, hook-and-eye at neck gorge, seam plain, two buttons at cuff, buttons flat, black silk lasting.

Pantaloons.

369. Black cloth, or doeskin cassimere, of uniform style.

Cloak.

370. A half-cloak—*á cavalier*—or cape of appropriate material, make, and color, emblazoned thereon, embroidered on proper colored cloth or velvet, the crest of the Order; to be worn over the left shoulder and back, fastened by a cord and tassel of appropriate color. The "gorget" worn with the same made of *three* triangular points; one of which will be *scarlet*, one *sky-blue*, and one *orange*. Pendant to the point of each proper color will be the appropriate letter, in *solid* white metal. The *gorget* to be separate, and fastened on by buttoning under collar of cape or by cord and tassel.

For members and subordinate officers, inclu-

UNIFORM.

Cloak.

sive of Worthy Chancellor: cloak *dark blue*, crest *scarlet.*

For Past Chancellors and Grand Officers, (of less rank than Grand Chancellor:) cloak *orange*, crest *blue.*

For Grand and Past Grand Chancellors: cloak *scarlet*, crest *blue.*

For Supreme and Past Supreme Chancellors: cloak *purple*, crest *gold.*

Helmet.

371. *White metal,* of lightest possible durable construction, regulation shape, wide scales

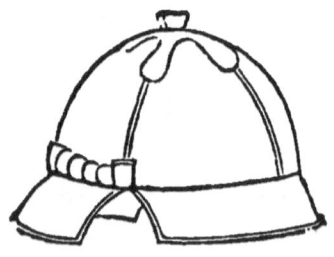 

and feather socket at the top, triangular in shape, with *point* of triangle to the front.

Plume.

372. In shape an oriflamme, of *three* stand-

UNIFORM.

Plume.

ing feathers, upper end curling to the front, and to be worn according to rank, as follows :

For Pages, *one* " blue " feather on front point of socket.

For Esquires, *one* " blue," *one* " yellow " feather at rear point of socket.

For Knights and subordinate Lodge officers, *one* " red," (at front point of socket,) *one* " yellow," *one* " blue " feather, (at rear points of socket.)

For Past Chancellors, *three* " blue " feathers.

For Grand Officers, *three* " yellow " feathers.

For Past Grand Chancellors, *three* " red " feathers, *en double or echelon.*

For Supreme and Past Supreme Chancellors, *three* " white " feathers, *en triple or echelon.*

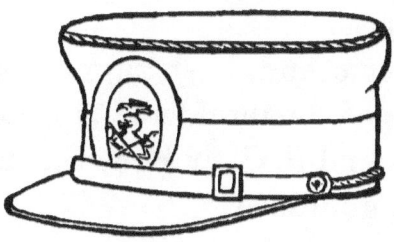

Cap.

373. Present navy style, black cloth, three to three and one-half inches height of crown, narrow, black leather straps fastened at sides with

UNIFORM.

Cap.

shield-shaped buttons. The crest or escutcheon of the Order on the front, and gold or silver lace running around the band of the cap, according to rank of wearer.

Escutcheon and Lace.

374. For Knights, Esquires, and Pages, silver-plated *metal*, shield-shaped escutcheon, and three linge silver lace.

For subordinate officers, inclusive of Worthy Chancellors, shield-shaped, embroidered escutcheon, on blue velvet and six linge silver lace.

For Grand Officers, inclusive of Grand Chancellor, shield-shaped, embroidered escutcheon, on orange velvet and nine linge silver lace.

For Past Grand Chancellors, oval-shaped, embroidered escutcheon, on red velvet and twelve linge gold lace.

For Supreme and Past Supreme Chancellors, circular-shaped, embroidered escutcheon, with vine around and S. C. or P. S. C., on purple and fifteen linge gold lace.

Baldric.

375. To be worn by all members of less rank than Grand Chancellors, five inches wide, in the whole, of blue, bordered with yellow, one

UNIFORM.

Baldric.

inch on either side, a strip of army lace one-fourth of an inch wide at the inner edge of the

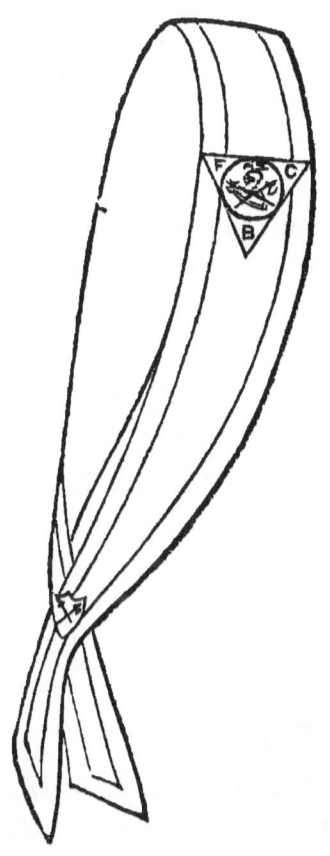

yellow. On the front centre of the baldric, a metal triangle with raised, or stuck up, escutcheon of the Order. On centre field of the triangle, and on each uncovered point thereof, one

UNIFORM.

Baldric.

of the letters "F., C., B.," so that the whole three may appear. The baldric to be worn from the right shoulder to the left hip, with ends extending six inches below the point of intersection, under and at the lower edge of the sword. belt, and be fastened with shield-shaped white metal screw button, the top of which will overlap the sword belt, and hold the baldric firmly in its place on the right shoulder.

Belt.

376. Red enamelled or patent leather two inches wide, fastened around the body with white metal clasp of emblematic design, two short, white metal chains suspended from red leather sliding straps on belt, and white metal slide, with hook, for fatigue cap.

Sword.

377. For all members and officers, (of less rank than Grand Chancellor,) thirty-four to forty inches long, white metal scabbard, cross handle, black hilt. Helmet head with appropriate devices, suspended by chains from two side rings.

For all officers and past officers, from rank of Grand Chancellor up, same as above, except gilt

UNIFORM.

Sword.

in place of white metal, and white instead of black grip.

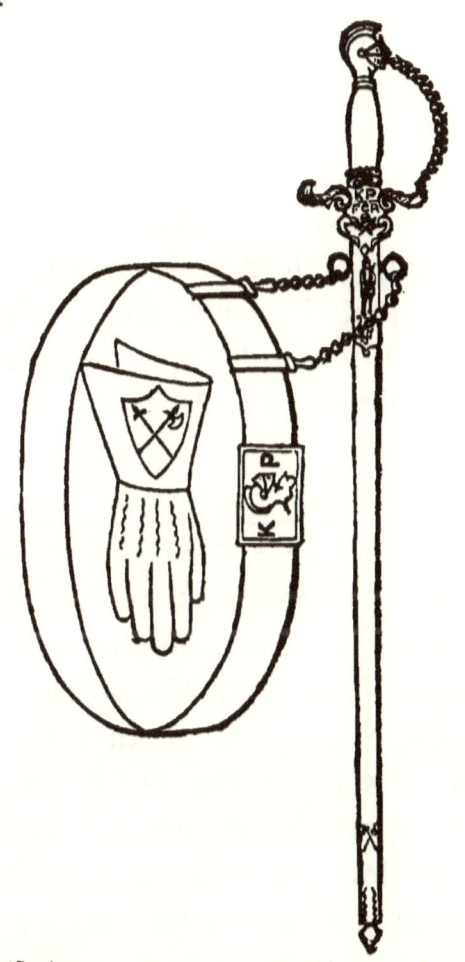

Gauntlets.

378. Black leather, military style, cuff to extend four and one-half inches up from its inter-

UNIFORM.

Gauntlets.

section with the hand, and to have a shield-shaped metal escutcheon of the Order (two inches in length) on back of cuff, or black kid gloves with patent leather cuffs, (of proper length and color,) separate or together, as most convenient to wearer, (and in fatigue dress, white gloves without the cuffs.) Knights, Chancellors, and Grand Officers, (of less rank than Grand Chancellor,) silver-plated escutcheons. Grand, Past Grand Chancellors, and Supreme and Past Supreme Chancellors, gold-plated escutcheons.

Shoulder-straps.

Supreme and Past Supreme Chancellors.

379. Royal purple silk velvet, four inches long by two inches wide, outside measurement, bordered with *three* rows of corded embroidery in gold, each one-eighth of an inch wide, the escutcheon or *crest* of the Order at each end, and a globe or world in centre. The Past Supreme Chancellors same as Supreme Chancellor, and to have in addition three small stars in silver, one at the centre of top, and one each at the right and left corners at the foot of the strap.

All the other Supreme Officers same size, color, and embroidery as Supreme Chancellor's,

UNIFORM.

Shoulder-straps.

Supreme and Past Supreme Chancellors.

UNIFORM.

Shoulder-straps.

Supreme and Past Supreme Chancellors.

with the exception of the escutcheon or crest at the ends, in place of which the initials (in old English characters) of their office, as equally divided as possible, at each end of the strap, all in gold.

Past Grand Chancellors.

380. Bright red silk velvet, four inches long by two inches wide, with *two* rows of corded embroidery each one-eighth of inch wide, and

escutcheon or crest of the Order embroidered in the middle *in gold,* and the letters "P. G. C." (in old English characters) embroidered *in silver* on the lower end of the strap.

Grand Chancellors.

381. Bright orange silk velvet, same size and embroidery as Past Grand Chancellor's, ex-

UNIFORM.

Shoulder-straps.

Grand Chancellors.

cept in centre is embroidered, in silver, a gaunt-let closed and grasping the truncheon of office,

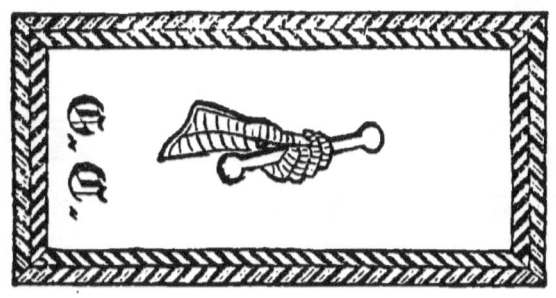

and at lower end of strap, *in silver,* (in old English characters,) the letters " G. C."

All other Grand Officers.

382. Same size, design, color, shape, and embroidery as Grand Chancellor's, except in centre of strap a shield, (instead of gauntlet, &c.,) and at the lower end (in old English characters) the initials of their office, but *all in silver.*

Past Chancellor.

383. Bright emerald green silk velvet, three and one-half inches long by one and one-half inches wide, bordered with one row of em-

UNIFORM.

Shoulder-straps.

Past Chancellor.

broidery, one-quarter inch wide, crossed battle-

axes in centre, and letters " P. C." (in old English) at lower end, all in silver.

Worthy Chancellor.

384. Bright blue silk velvet, same size and
design as Past Chancellor in other respects, except in centre is embroidered, in silver, crossed
swords and a hand-lance in gold, running length-

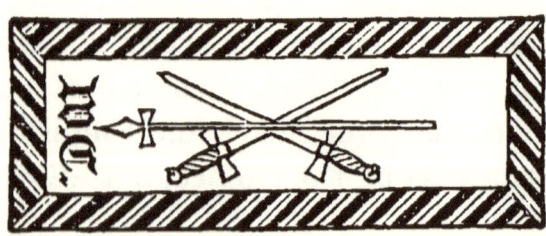

wise of the strap through the swords, head towards the foot, and the letters " W. C." (in old
English characters) at the foot of the strap, in
silver.

UNIFORM.

Shoulder-straps.

Vice Chancellor.

385. The same as Worthy Chancellor, except, instead of crossed swords in centre, is simply a tilting lance, running lengthwise, head

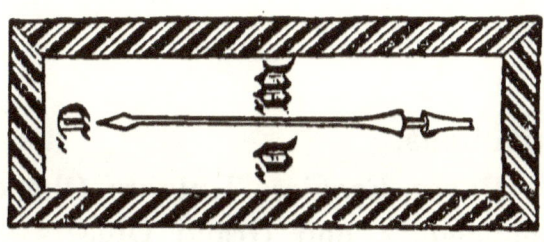

towards the foot of strap, and letters " W." and " V." in centre, on either side of lance, and " C." at foot of the same, covered by head of the lance, all in silver.

Other Subordinate Lodge Officers.

386. Same as Worthy Chancellor and Vice Chancellor in color, and embroidery on edges ; no design, but with simply the letters (in old English) or initials indicative of the various officers in triangular arrangement in the centre.

Arms.

387. For Page, battle-axe and shield, of appropriate make and material.

UNIFORM.

Arms.

For Esquires, lance and shield, of appropriate make and material.

For Knights, sword and shield, as prescribed, and of appropriate make and material.

For officers and past officers, swords, as heretofore prescribed.

Distinctions.

388. Pages, Esquires, Knights, Chancellors, Past Chancellors, and Grand Officers (of less rank than Grand Chancellor) will wear *white metal* or *silver* wherever metal, embroidery, or lace appears, unless otherwise specifically stated. Grand and Past Grand Chancellors, Supreme and Past Supreme Officers, *yellow metal* or *gold* wherever metal, embroidery, or lace appears, unless otherwise specifically stated.

VACANCIES.

389. In case of vacancies in office, it is perfectly legal for the Lodge to nominate, elect, and install into said office, on one and the same evening, a properly qualified member of the Lodge.

VICE CHANCELLOR.

390. The Vice Chancellor shall be elected semi-annually at the last stated meetings of the term.

391. He shall assist the Worthy Chancellor in preserving order in the Lodge, and aid him in conducting the ceremonies.

392. He shall appoint a minority of all Committees, unless otherwise ordered by the Lodge.

393. He shall have charge of the wicket.

394. He shall preside in the absence of the Worthy Chancellor, and perform such other duties appertaining to his office as are enjoined by the laws, rules, and regulations.

395. To qualify a member for the office of Vice Chancellor, he shall have been legally elected to and served in the office of Guide.

VISITORS.

396. A Past Chancellor who is present as a visitor in a Lodge has no privileges beyond those of any other visiting brother. He cannot claim the right, on account of his rank in the Order, to address the Lodge on any subject whatever. The Lodge may confer the privilege for the occasion, or may extend an invitation to any

VISITORS.

member of the Order who has attained the Knight's degree to address the Lodge.

VOTE.

397. It is not legal for a Lodge to pass a law preventing a brother from speaking or voting on the night of his admission as a Knight.

398. In voting upon any question before a Lodge, the Worthy Chancellor may require every member present to vote, unless excused by the Lodge; but when such requirement is not made by the Worthy Chancellor or the Lodge, no notice can be taken of members not voting, (further than their tacit agreement with the majority voting,) and when there are no votes in opposition to a question, it is unanimously carried within the meaning of any law that would require a unanimous vote.

399. The Worthy Chancellor is not entitled to vote except on the election of officers, or on any vote taken by ballot, or in cases where there are only seven members present, when he is required to vote, or when the Lodge is equally divided on a question, when he shall have the casting vote. A vote by ballot resulting in a tie cannot be decided by the Worthy Chancellor, but must be renewed until a decision is obtained.

VOTE.

400. At an election for officers of a subordinate Lodge, no votes shall be counted, except for candidates legally nominated; consequently a blank vote cannot be counted.

401. When a division upon a vote is called, the Worthy Chancellor may require the brothers to rise on their feet, but each one voting must give the voting sign, in order to be counted by the Guide, and when the Guide has counted the affirmative and negative vote and reported to the Worthy Chancellor, it is too late for any brother to claim a right to vote.

402. All members in good standing have a right to vote for Representative to the Grand Lodge.

403. The vote is required to be taken with ball ballots in the following cases, viz.:

1. Upon a report of a Committee on candidate for initiation.

2. Upon a report of a Committee on application on card.

3. Upon the report of a Committee on application to restore a member suspended for non-payment of dues.

4. Upon the report of a Committee on charges, as to the guilt or innocence of the accused.

VOTE.

5. To determine the punishment to be inflicted upon a brother found guilty as charged.

404. When there is but one nomination for an office, it is perfectly legal for the Lodge to direct the Worthy Chancellor to cast the vote of the Lodge for the nominee.

405. At an election for Grand Lodge officers upon the floor of the Grand Lodge, none but Representatives are entitled to vote.

406. A decision of the Chair being appealed from, the question put, "Shall the decision of the Chair be sustained?" and the vote resulting in a tie, neither the Worthy Chancellor nor the Vice Chancellor (who put the question) having voted, it is the duty of the Vice Chancellor to announce that the decision of the Chair is not sustained.

407. To draw an order for weekly benefits, a motion must be made in proper form, and a vote taken thereon.

408. It requires two-thirds of all the valid votes cast to adopt or amend the By-Laws, to appropriate or expend money, remove an officer, reinstate, restore, fine, or suspend a member.

409. A vote by Lodges shall be taken upon

VOTE.

any question before the Grand Lodge at the call
of three Representatives.

VOUCHING.

410. Members of the Order desirous of visiting Lodges, and deficient in the work, cannot
be vouched for by other members.

WIDOWS' AND ORPHANS' FUND.

411. A Lodge having a Widows' and Orphans' Fund, also a by-law providing for a
special board of trustees for said fund, cannot
place any sum or sums of the above-named fund
in the hands or at the disposal of the trustees
for the general fund.

WORK.

412. A Lodge is not lawfully opened, or
legally at work, unless the charter thereof is in
the Lodge, or ante-room under the control of the
Lodge; nor unless there is a copy of the Holy
Bible upon the altar of the Lodge, or at the
position of the Venerable Patriarch.

413. A subordinate Lodge cannot decide
any question relating to the work of the Order.
The work emanates from the Supreme Lodge,
and is conveyed by the Grand Representatives

WORK.

to the Grand Lodge, where it is imparted to the Representatives of the subordinate Lodges, the District Deputy Grand Chancellors, Grand Lodge officers, or the Committee of Superintendence, who instruct the subordinates. In the absence of a District Deputy Grand Chancellor, a Grand Lodge officer, or the Committee of Superintendence, the instructions of the Representatives must be conformed to.

414. Any subordinate Lodge which may cause to be printed, for their own or other use, any of the private work of the Order, upon satisfactory proof thereof, shall be suspended, and forfeit their charter.

WORTHY CHANCELLOR.

415. The Worthy Chancellor shall be elected semi-annually, at the last stated meetings of the term.

416. It is his duty to preside at all meetings of the Lodge, and preserve decorum therein; enforce the laws, rules, and regulations of the Lodge, and those of the Grand Lodge.

417. He shall decide all questions of order without debate, subject to an appeal to the Lodge by any member.

WORTHY CHANCELLOR.

418. He shall appoint the majority of all Committees, unless otherwise ordered by the Lodge.

419. He shall sign all orders on the Banker for such moneys as may be ordered by a vote of the Lodge to be paid.

420. He shall receive the money drawn for benefits, and cause the same to be paid to the person for whom it was drawn within forty-eight hours thereafter.

421. He shall decide who is entitled to the floor when two or more members rise to speak at the same time.

422. He shall perform all such duties as are enjoined by the laws, rules, and regulations of the Order.

423. To qualify a member for the office of Worthy Chancellor, he shall have been legally elected to and served in the office of Vice Chancellor.

424. A Worthy Chancellor, against whom charges are pending at the end of his term of office, is not entitled to take his seat as Venerable Patriarch, nor does he become a Past Chancellor; and the Lodge must withhold his

WORTHY CHANCELLOR.

Past Chancellor's certificate until the charges are disposed of.

YEAS AND NAYS.

425. On the call of five Representatives, the yeas and nays shall be taken on any question before the Grand Lodge, and entered on the Journal.

RULES.

When any of the rules, adopted by the assembly, or in force, relative to its manner of proceeding, is disregarded or infringed, every member has the right to take notice thereof, and to require that the presiding officer, or any other whose duty it is, shall carry such rule into execution; and, in that case, the rule must be enforced at once, without debate or delay. It is then too late to alter, repeal, or suspend the rule; so long as any one member insists upon its execution, it must be enforced.

PRESIDING OFFICER.

The presiding officer may read sitting; but should rise to state a motion, or put a question to the assembly.

DECORUM.

The observance of decorum by the members of a deliberative assembly is not only due to themselves and to one another, as gentlemen assembled together to deliberate on matters of common

DECORUM.

importance and interest, but is also essential to
the regular and satisfactory proceeding of such
an assembly. The rules on this subject, though
generally laid down with reference to decorum
in debate, are equally applicable whether the
assembly be at the time engaged in debate or
not; and therefore it may be stated, generally,
that no member is to disturb another, or the
assembly itself, by hissing, coughing, or spitting;
by speaking or whispering to other members;
by standing up to the interruption of others; by
passing between the presiding officer and a member speaking; going across the assembly room,
or walking up and down in it; taking books or
papers from the table, or writing there.

DIVISION OF A QUESTION.

When a proposition or motion is complicated,
that is, composed of two or more parts which
are so far independent of each other as to be
susceptible of division into several questions, and
it is supposed that the assembly may approve
of some but not of all these parts, it is a com-
pendious mode of amendment to divide the motion into separate questions, to be separately
voted upon and decided by the assembly.

When a motion for a division is made, the

DIVISION OF A QUESTION.

mover ought to specify in his motion the manner in which he proposes to make the division; and this motion, like every other of the nature of an amendment, is itself susceptible of amendment.

MODIFICATION OF A MOTION.

The mover of a proposition is sometimes allowed to modify it, after it has been stated as a question by the presiding officer; but, as this is equivalent to a withdrawal of the motion, in order to substitute another in its place, and since a motion regularly made, seconded, and proposed cannot be withdrawn without leave, it is clear that the practice alluded to rests only upon common consent; and that, if objected to, the mover of a proposition must obtain the permission of the assembly, by a motion and question for the purpose, in order to enable him to modify his proposition.

QUESTION OF ORDER.

It is the right of every member, taking notice of the breach of a rule, to insist upon the enforcement of it.

When a question of order is raised, as it may be by any one member, it is not stated from the chair, and decided by the assembly, like other

QUESTION OF ORDER.

questions; but is decided in the first instance by the presiding officer, without any previous debate or discussion by the assembly. If the decision of the presiding officer is not satisfactory, any one member may object to it, and have the question decided by the assembly. This is called "appealing" from the decision of the Chair. On an appeal the presiding officer is allowed to take part in the debate, which, on ordinary occasions, he is prohibited from doing.

LIE ON THE TABLE.

A motion to lie on the table is usually resorted to, when the assembly has something else before it, which claims its present attention, and therefore desires to lay aside a proposition for a short but indefinite time, reserving to itself the power to take it up when convenient. This motion takes precedence of and supersedes all the other subsidiary motions.

"If decided in the affirmative, the principal motion, together with all the other motions, subsidiary and incidental, connected with it, is removed from before the assembly, until it is again taken up, which it may be, by motion and vote, at any time when the assembly pleases."

SPEAKING.

It is customary for the presiding officer, after a motion has been made, seconded, and proposed, to give the floor to the mover, in preference to others, if he rises to speak; or, on resuming a debate after an adjournment, to give the floor, if he desires it, to the mover of the adjournment, in preference to other members; or, where two or more members claim the floor, to prefer him who is opposed to the measure in question; but, in all these cases, the determination of the presiding officer may be overruled by the assembly.

It is sometimes supposed that, because a member has a right to explain himself, he therefore has a right to interrupt another member whilst speaking, in order to make the explanation: but this is a mistake; he should wait until the member speaking has finished; and if a member, on being requested, yields the floor for an explanation, he relinquishes it altogether.

QUESTION.

When any proposition is made to a deliberative assembly it is called a *motion;* when it is stated or propounded to the assembly for their acceptance or rejection it is denominated a *question;* and when adopted it becomes the *order, resolution,* or *vote* of the assembly.

COMMITTEE OF THE WHOLE.

When a subject has been ordered to be referred to a Committee of the Whole, the form of going from the assembly into Committee is for the presiding officer, at the time appointed for the Committee to sit, on motion made and seconded for the purpose, to put the question that the assembly do now resolve itself into a Committee of the Whole, to take under consideration such a matter, naming it. If this question is determined in the affirmative, the result is declared by the presiding officer, who, naming some member to act as Chairman of the Committee, then leaves the chair, and takes a seat elsewhere, like any other member; and the person appointed Chairman seats himself (not in the chair of the assembly but) at the clerk's table.

The Chairman named by the presiding officer is generally acquiesced in by the Committee; though, like all other Committees, a Committee of the Whole have a right to elect a Chairman for themselves, some member, by general consent, putting the question.

The same number of members is necessary to constitute a quorum of a Committee of the Whole as of the assembly; and if the members present fall below a quorum at any time in the

COMMITTEE OF THE WHOLE.

course of the proceedings, the Chairman, on a motion and question, rises—the presiding officer thereupon resumes the chair—and the Chairman informs the assembly (he can make no other report) of the cause of the dissolution of the Committee.

When the assembly is in Committee of the Whole, it is the duty of the presiding officer to remain in the assembly-room, in order to be at hand to resume the chair in case the Committee should be broken up by some disorder, or for want of a quorum, or should rise, either to report progress or to make their final report upon the matter committed to them.

The clerk of the assembly does not act as clerk of the Committee, (this is the duty of the assistant clerk in legislative bodies,) or record in his journal any of the proceedings or votes of the Committee, but only their report as made to the assembly.

The proceedings in a Committee of the Whole, though in general similar to those in the assembly itself and in other Committees, are yet different in some respects, the principal of which are the following:

First. The previous question cannot be moved in a Committee of the Whole. The only means

COMMITTEE OF THE WHOLE.

of avoiding an improper discussion is to move that the Committee rise; and, if it is apprehended that the same discussion will be attempted on returning again into Committee, the assembly can discharge the Committee, and proceed itself with the business, keeping down any improper discussion by means of the previous question.*

Second. A Committee of the Whole cannot adjourn, like other Committees, to some other time or place, for the purpose of going on with and completing the consideration of the subject referred to them; but, if their business is unfinished at the usual time for the assembly to adjourn, or for any other reason they wish to proceed no further at a particular time, the form of proceeding is for some member to move that the Committee rise, report progress, and ask leave to sit again; and, if this motion prevails, the Chairman rises, the presiding officer resumes the chair of the assembly, and the Chairman of the Committee informs him that the Committee of the Whole have, according to

---

* If the object be to stop debate, that can only be effected in the same manner, unless there is a special rule as to the time of speaking, or to taking a subject out of Committee.

COMMITTEE OF THE WHOLE.

order, had under their consideration such a matter, and have made some progress therein,* but not having had time to go through with the same, have directed him to ask leave for the Committee to sit again. The presiding officer thereupon puts a question on giving the Committee leave to sit again, and also on the time when the assembly will again resolve itself into a Committee. If leave to sit again is not granted, the Committee is of course dissolved.

Third. In a Committee of the Whole every member may speak as often as he pleases, provided he can obtain the floor; whereas, in the assembly itself, no member can speak more than once.

Fourth. A Committee of the Whole cannot refer any matter to another Committee; but other Committees may and do frequently exercise their functions, and expedite their business by means of sub-committees of their own members.

Fifth. In a Committee of the Whole the presiding officer of the assembly has a right to take a part in the debate and proceedings, in the same manner as any other member.

---

* If it is a second time, the expression is "some further progress," &c.

13

COMMITTEE OF THE WHOLE.

Sixth. A Committee of the Whole, like a Select Committee, has no authority to punish a breach of order, whether of a member or stranger; but can only rise and report the matter to the assembly, who may proceed to punish the offender. Disorderly words must be written down in Committee, in the same manner as in the assembly, and reported to the assembly for their animadversion.

The foregoing are the principal points of difference between proceedings in the assembly and in Committees of the Whole; in most other respects they are precisely similar. It is sometimes said that in a Committee of the Whole it is not necessary that a motion should be seconded. There is no foundation, however, either in reason or parliamentary usage, for this opinion.

When a Committee of the Whole have gone through with the matter referred to them, a member moves that the Committee rise, and that the Chairman (or some other member) report their proceedings to the assembly; which being resolved, the Chairman rises and goes to his place, the presiding officer resumes the chair of the assembly, and the Chairman informs him that the Committee have gone through with the

COMMITTEE OF THE WHOLE.

business referred to them, and that he is ready to make their report when the assembly shall think proper to receive it. The time for receiving the report is then agreed upon; and, at the time appointed, it is made and received in the same manner as that of any other Committee.

SUGGESTIONS TO PRESIDING OFFICERS.

One of the most essential parts of the duty of a presiding officer is to give the closest attention to the proceedings of the assembly, and especially to what is said by every member who speaks. Without the first, confusion will be almost certain to occur, wasting the time, perhaps disturbing the harmony of the assembly. The latter is not merely a decent manifestation of respect for those who have elevated him to an honorable station, but it tends greatly to encourage timid or diffident members, and to secure them a patient and attentive hearing; and it often enables the presiding officer, by a timely interference, to check offensive language in season to prevent scenes of tumult and disorder, such as have sometimes disgraced our legislative halls.

It should be constantly kept in mind by a

SUGGESTIONS TO PRESIDING OFFI-CERS.

presiding officer that in a deliberative assembly there can regularly be but one thing done or doing at the same time. This caution he will find particularly useful to him whenever a quarrel arises between two members, in consequence of words spoken in debate. In such a case, he will do well to require that the regular course of proceedings shall be strictly pursued, and will take care to restrain members from interfering in any other manner. In general, the solemnity and deliberation with which this mode is attended will do much to allay heat and excitement, and to restore harmony and order to the assembly.

A presiding officer will often find himself embarrassed by the difficulty as well as the delicacy of deciding points of order, or giving directions as to the manner of proceeding. In such cases it will be useful for him to recollect that—

The great purpose of all rules and forms is to subserve the will of the assembly rather than to restrain it; to facilitate, and not to obstruct the expression of their deliberate sense.

PETITIONS.

When a petition has been received, the next step in the proceedings is the reading of it by

PETITIONS.

the clerk, for the information of the assembly; which, though in the usual course of business, and not likely to be objected to after the petition has been received, is nevertheless the subject of a motion and question, to be regularly submitted to the assembly and voted upon; and, until a petition has been read, no order can properly be made respecting it—not even for its lying on the table.

INTERRUPTION OF A MEMBER SPEAKING.

The rule stated that a member speaking cannot rightfully be interrupted in his speech but by a call to order, does not make it the duty of the presiding officer to refuse to hear a member who rises and addresses the Chair whilst another is speaking; for if this were the case, the presiding officer could very rarely know whether there might not be occasion for the interruption, and would thus be in danger of keeping the assembly in ignorance of matters which it might be of the highest concern for them to know. When, therefore, a member rises whilst another is speaking, and addresses the Chair, he should inform the presiding officer that he rises to a point of order, or to the orders of the

INTERRUPTION OF A MEMBER SPEAKING.

assembly, or to a matter of privilege. It will then be the duty of the presiding officer to direct the member speaking to suspend his remarks or to resume his seat, and the member rising to proceed with the statement of his point or other matter of order, or of privilege. If the latter on proceeding discloses matter which shows that the interruption was proper, the subject so introduced must first be disposed of, and then the member who was interrupted is to be directed to proceed with his speech. If it appears that there was no sufficient ground for the interruption, the member rising is to be directed to resume his seat, and the member interrupted to proceed with his speech. Every member, therefore, possessing the right to interrupt another in his speech on a proper occasion, any wanton abuse of this right, for the purpose of personal annoyance, is liable to censure and punishment; it being itself a breach of order unnecessarily and wantonly to call or interrupt another member to order.

In reference to the occasions on which the interruption of a member speaking is allowed, it is to be observed that they are not restricted to breaches of order in debate on the part of the

INTERRUPTION OF A MEMBER SPEAK-ING.

member speaking.   Any matter of privilege affecting the assembly itself or any of its members, of which the assembly ought to have instant information, furnishes such an occasion; as, for example, where access to the place of sitting of the assembly is obstructed, or the person of a member is attacked; or where something connected with the proceeding of the assembly requires instant attention, as where it becomes necessary to have lights; or where something occurs relative to the member himself who is speaking, as where he is annoyed and disturbed by noise and disorder; or where, in consequence of his strength failing him, it becomes necessary that he should finish his speech sitting.

REPORT OF COMMITTEE.

The report of a Committee being the conclusion which is agreed to by a majority of the members, the dissenting or not-agreeing members, according to strict parliamentary practice, would have no other mode of bringing their views before the assembly than as individual members.   Inasmuch, however, as such members may be supposed to have given the subject

REPORT OF COMMITTEE.

equal consideration with the other members of the Committee, and may, therefore, be in possession of views and opinions equally worthy of the attention of the assembly, the practice has become general in the legislative assemblies of this country to allow members in the minority to present their views and conclusions in the parliamentary form of a report, which is accordingly known by the somewhat incongruous appellation of a minority report. Any two or more of the members may unite in such a report, or each one of them may express his views in a separate document.

A minority report is not recognized as a report of the Committee, or acted upon as such; it is received by courtesy, and allowed to accompany the report as representing the opinions of the minority; and, in order to its being adopted by the assembly, it must be moved as an amendment to the report, when that comes to be considered.

FORMS.

PAST CHANCELLOR'S CERTIFICATE.

To the Grand Lodge of Pa., K. of P.:

.... *Lodge, No...*

THIS IS TO CERTIFY, That P. C. ......, having been duly qualified, passed the W. C's chair of this Lodge, being clear of the books, and under no charge, is thereby entitled to become a member of the Grand Lodge of Pennsylvania.

In witness whereof, We have hereunto set our hands and affixed the seal of the Lodge, this .... day of ...., A. D. 18.., at ......

[SEAL.]

...., W. C.

Attest:

...., R. S.

FORMS.

REPRESENTATIVE'S CERTIFICATE.

To the Grand Lodge of Pa., K. of P.:

.... *Lodge, No.* ..

THIS IS TO CERTIFY, That P. C. ...... has been duly elected the Representative of this Lodge, to serve from the .... Tuesday in ...., 18.., until the .... Tuesday in ...., 18..

In witness whereof, We have hereunto set our hands and affixed the seal of the Lodge, this .... day of ...., A. D. 18.., at .....

............., W. C.

[SEAL.]

Attest:

............., R. S.

FORMS.

TRANSFER CERTIFICATE.

To the Grand Lodge of Pa., K. of P.:

.... *Lodge, No.* ...

THIS IS TO CERTIFY, That P. C. ......, formerly of .... Lodge, No. .., K. of P. of ......, has deposited his card in this Lodge, is clear on the books, and under no charge, and therefore entitled to membership in the Grand Lodge.

In witness whereof, We have hereunto set our hands and affixed the seal of the Lodge, this .... day of ...., A. D. 18.., at ....

.............., W. C.

.............., R. S.

[SEAL.]

Attest:

FORMS.

PAST CHANCELLOR'S CERTIFICATE BY DISPENSATION.

To the Grand Lodge of Pa., K. of P.:

.... *Lodge, No.* ..

THIS IS TO CERTIFY, That P. C. ......, having served a term as ...... of this Lodge, without compensation, being clear on the books, and under no charge, is fully qualified to become a member of the Grand Lodge of Pennsylvania.

In witness whereof, We have hereunto set our hands and affixed the seal of the Lodge, this .... day of ...., A. D. 18.., at ....

...., W. C.

[SEAL.]

Attest:

...., R. S.

FORMS.

APPLICATION FOR CHARTER.

To the Grand Lodge of Pa., K. of P.:

The undersigned, residing in ......, county of ......, respectfully petition your honorable body to grant them a Charter or Dispensation to establish a Lodge of the Knights of Pythias, to be located in ......; said Lodge to be known as ...... Lodge, No. ..., of Knights of Pythias, and under your jurisdiction.

Charter fee enclosed, $...

Dated, ..., A. D. 18..

Signed, ...

      ....

      ....

14

FORMS.

APPLICATION FOR MEMBERSHIP.

................................, 18..

To the Officers and Members of

.... *Lodge, No. .., K. of P.:*

Having conceived a favorable impression of your honorable Order, I herewith present myself as a candidate for initiation.

If accepted, I promise a full and due observance of all laws that govern the Lodge.

Signature...

Age........

Residence...

Occupation..

Recommended by Bro. Kt.................................

Bro. Kt.................................

Fee enclosed, $........

FORMS.

APPLICATION FOR MEMBERSHIP ON CARD.

..............., 18..

To the Officers and Members of

.... Lodge, No. .., *K. of P.:*

Having conceived a favorable impression of your Lodge, I herewith present myself a candidate for membership.

If accepted, I promise a full and due observance of all laws governing the Lodge.

Enclosed find my Withdrawal Card from .... Lodge, No. ..

Signature.................

Age.......

Residence.................

Occupation.................

Recommended by Bro. Kt..............

Bro. Kt..............

Fee enclosed, $.......

ANALYTICAL INDEX.

(161)

SECTION.

15

INDEX

TO

SELECTIONS FROM CUSHING'S MANUAL,

FORMS, &c.